I0683509

three cOUrses

Short Stories from Creative Writing Modules

Philip Wadner

2015

Published by Cade Books

©2015 Philip Wadner

All rights reserved.

ISBN 978-0-9931987-3-1

Philip Wadner has asserted his right under the Copyright, Designs and Patents Act 1988 to be identified as the author of this work.

This book is sold subject to the condition that it shall not, by way of trade or otherwise, be lent, resold, hired out, or otherwise circulated without the publisher's prior consent in any form of binding or cover other than that in which it is published and without a similar condition, including this condition, being imposed on the subsequent purchaser.

www.cadebooks.co.uk

Contents

Preface..1

Short Stories 3

    Photo Finish 5

    Steamy Nights 15

    Modern Babylon..23

    Chocolate Surprise 35

    The Lift..45

    Haunted Dreams..49

    The Blue Suit...57

    Eyes in the Back of her Head..63

    The Last Picnic..69

    Spoiled Pig 73

    Wedding Blues 77

    Full Circle..83

Life Writing..87

    The Man with a Smile 89

    Two Minutes Silence...97

    Penny Bridge 101

Micro Fiction..121

    Rescue Me 123

    Greasy Spoon 124

    Faith..125

    Haggis Supper 126

    Doggone 127

    Sisters 128

    CCTV 129

    Freedom at Last...130

    Number Four Cake...131

    The Green Man 132

Preface

For many people, early retirement is not an option. I was lucky. After forty years in engineering I decided to break out, and embarked upon a BA(Hons) with the Open University to see whether Arts could be as challenging as Science. Writing was not new to me. I had produced enough technical proposals, engineering reports, journal articles, patent applications and scientific presentations to fill a good-sized skip. But 'Creative Writing'? Some of my colleagues would doubtless argue that much of what I had previously written had indeed been creative, but not in an 'Arty' way!

Back in 2010, the Open University offered three courses in creative writing. An entry level module, A174 Start Writing Fiction provided a gentle introduction. That course is no longer available. At level 2, A215 Creative Writing ramped up the demands at an alarming rate and any thoughts that writing fiction was an easy option compared to say rocket science were soon dashed. Although the Level 3 module A363 Advanced Creative Writing had a shorter course text, it explored poetry and fiction in new forms and in greater depth. Together they presented a considerable challenge and three years of tough, but incredibly satisfying, study.

So, why publish this collection?

For writing to be 'creative' it requires a reader. A story is surely no more than a collection of printed words until it is read. It is the reader who takes the words and conjures up meaning in their mind. It might not be what the writer intended, and more than one reader may find different meanings. But that doesn't matter. The circle has been completed.

The stories I have included are taken across the board from all three modules. They have not been chosen on literary merit (whatever that is). The ones selected are here mostly because I smiled when I read them again, but also because I have tried to embrace a range of genres and subjects to give the best chance of pleasing a wide readership.

I hope you enjoy the collection.

Phil Wadner, July 2015

Following valuable feedback from readers after publication, I have made some minor revisions to the stories 'Full Circle' and 'Two Minutes Silence'.

Phil Wadner, September 2015

Short Stories

Photo Finish

Alex stopped breathing the instant the child's cry filtered down the stairway. Instinctively she touched the button on her head torch, plunging the lounge into darkness. Using the silhouette of the photo frames to guide her to the sideboard, she reached forward and picked up the watches, taking care not to let them slip to the floor from between her gloved fingers. Placing them inside the large pocket sewn into her charcoal jacket, she listened carefully, her soft plimsolls frozen to the carpet. A floorboard creaked overhead, and a small bead of sweat appeared on her forehead followed by another, then another. A latch clicked, and a faint triangle of light appeared at the lounge door which could only mean that the landing light had been switched on.

'Shush, shush. I'm coming,' said a distant voice.

Footsteps creaked along the landing.

'Daddy's here. What's the matter, little man?'

Alex didn't wait a moment longer and walked quickly along the dimly lit hall to the kitchen. She stepped silently through the door, disappearing into the gloom.

Another night of broken sleep. Brian switched on the kitchen television hoping that the morning news bulletin would give him something different to think about. It was early. Much too early to start the day. But BJ had kept on crying until Brian gave in and let him ride piggyback down the stairs to the kitchen table. He hit the remote for a cartoon channel.

'Just take it easy with the Frosties, young man.'

But it was too late, and BJ aimed a spoonful at the mouse on the television.

'Now, what did I just tell you?'

This was not the best day for Brian's temper to be tested. The one date he would always remember without having to check his diary. In a short four hours time, it would be three years, to the minute, the second, that changed their lives forever.

Brian stared at the television, the hullabaloo affording no distraction to his thoughts.

How can it be that long? Three years. And it's still a blur. A dark stain. Friends try to wash it out, but it comes back. Stubborn. Deep-seated. If only it was just the burgundy red of spilled wine. Or the yellow ochre of a dropped egg. Or the cocoa brown of melted chocolate. But it's not. It's an unforgiving black. I want to undo that fatal second. Anything it takes. I ache to hear her sigh when I drop toast on the floor, to smell her fragrance lingering in the bedroom, and to feel her sweet breath on my lips.

BJ banged his spoon on the rim of the empty bowl.

'Daddy, you've gone to that place again.' BJ gave an exaggerated sigh. 'What can we do today? Something exciting?'

'How would you like to go and play with your cousin at Auntie's, and stay the night?'

Brian lifted BJ off his chair and held him high above his head. The three-year-old giggled.

'I'll take that as a yes, then. Come on, get dressed and we'll drive over there. Daddy's going out later.'

Brian cleared his throat as he made his way up the narrow stairway leading from the public bar to the functions room. The higher he climbed, the stronger the smell. There was a familiarity he couldn't place, and then out of the blue it came to him. The cocktail of perfume, aftershave and alcohol took him back to the clubs of his teenage years.

The door at the top of the stairs was held ajar by a large spirits bottle filled with coins, light jazz spilling onto the landing. Brian paused at the opening.

'Everything OK, sir?' asked the girl seated behind a small table just inside. 'Do you have a ticket?'

'Er, yes, hang on.'

Brian took out his wallet and found the ticket, but instead of taking it out he fumbled around looking through the compartments.

'What am I doing, coming to a place like this?' he mumbled into his wallet.

He started to turn away, but a head of black curls appeared out of nowhere, grabbed his hand and dragged him inside.

'Haven't seen you here before, have I?' said the girl, pulling Brian towards the bar.

'My name's Brian. And yes, this is... this is my first time.' Brian paused, and looked down at the floor. 'Coming to a single's night, I mean.'

'Well, First Time Brian. How about buying me a drink?'

People were queuing at the bar, but the girl managed to push her way through to the front.

'Usual please, barman,' she called. 'And a pint of lager for Brian.'

'Not sure I'm in a lager mood tonight,' said Brian, shallow frown lines creasing his forehead.

The girl shrugged, turned away and wrapped an arm around a smartly-suited chap perched on a high stool.

Backing away from the bar, Brian looked around the dimly lit room. A raised platform at the opposite end to the bar was set out with karaoke gear, large speakers sounding out the offbeat rhythm of an old Dave Brubeck number. A brick fireplace played artificial flames across the hearth.

Brian could see a low table tucked away in the corner near the fireplace, and made his way towards it, checking that the girl with the black curls wasn't following him. He had sat down before he realised that the table was occupied.

'Oh, sorry, I didn't see you there,' he said.

The woman wore a dark hooded top and was reaching down to a large bag next to her chair. She glanced up.

'That's OK, no worries. I was just about to leave anyway.'

Her voice blended perfectly with the music. Brian had heard that soft lilt before. He wanted her to say something else.

'Well, don't let me push you out.'

'Like I said, I was going.'

Half a dozen simple words, but spoken in a quiet self-assured manner he hadn't heard in three years.

'No. Please. Stay.' Brian quickly sat down opposite her. 'This is my first time here and I could really do with someone to chat with.'

He realised how weak that sounded, and began to stand up. The young woman pushed her hood back and relaxed into her seat.

'OK, just for a few minutes,' she purred, 'but I do need to get home, and...'

'And what?' asked Brian, pleased to have the opportunity to hear more of her voice.

'Well, to be honest, I have to get some sleep.'

Brian raised his eyebrows.

'Well, I work nights. Early mornings, actually. So this is late for me.' She laughed. 'Doesn't that sound feeble? I'm more worried about sleep than having a good time.'

The light from the fire flickered across the young woman's hair as Brian allowed her soft voice to melt into his subconscious. She looked up from the table, and when he saw her face clearly for the first time, it was Brian's turn to slump back into his chair. Her eyes were like magnets, charged spheres, dark dangerous whirlpools. He tried to swim away but felt he was being sucked inside.

'Sorry, I don't mean to stare.' Brian's gaze was fixed on the face across the table.

'Then why are you?' Her eyes turned away for an instant before returning to play their magic once again.

'You remind me so much of someone. The tone of your voice, the colour of your hair, your eyes. It's so uncanny.'

The young woman laughed.

'Well, I can't say it's the first time I've heard that old line,' she said.

Brian shook his head slowly, grimacing at how clumsy he must have sounded.

'Might have known I'd show myself up. It was the lads. They thought I should try a singles bar.'

Brian told her about the girl with black curls, looking around to check she wasn't about to pounce.

'Not the best start to the evening, then,' she said, 'and I didn't mean to make you feel awkward.'

Reaching across the table, she swept her fingers playfully over his.

'Anyway, you've done better than I have. Been sitting here for two hours and you're the first person to talk to me. Oh, and even that was accidental since you thought the table was empty.'

Brian smiled, his shoulders dropping a little as he settled down into the soft leather chair.

'Would you like a drink?' he asked.

'No thanks, I really do need to be getting home.'

Brian pulled up the sleeve of his jacket.

'Oh, forgot, no watch.'

'Lose it, or just forget to put it on?' she asked.

'I think I've lost it, although I'm not sure. That sounds daft, doesn't it? No, this morning it wasn't on the sideboard where I always leave it overnight. Next to my wife's. Between photographs of her and our son. We bought each other a special watch to celebrate his birth. Actually, I can't remember seeing hers there either.'

'Could someone have moved them?'

'To be honest, I was so preoccupied at the time I didn't give it much thought. And BJ, that's our son, Brian Junior, I'm Brian by the way, was excited about spending the night with his cousin and I needed to pack his things and drive him over there. Maybe I just popped the watches in a drawer. Unless they were stolen in the night. But, come on. A burglar doing the rounds in our run-down part of town? That'll be the day.'

Brian laughed, and looked for some shared reaction, but it didn't come.

'I'm sure I'd have woken up if anyone was in the house. Last night BJ was a bit upset and I heard him cry straight away. No, they'll be in the drawer.'

'What happened? Your wife, I mean.'

Brian closed his eyes and breathed slowly through pursed lips, recalling the event for what felt the millionth time.

'I couldn't believe that at last we were taking BJ home,' he said quietly. 'We'd been backwards and forwards to the hospital for days.'

Brian paused, looking into space, reliving the moment. He could see the rear view mirror, and reflected in it his wife's startlingly beautiful face, flaxen locks falling across deep chestnut eyes as she watched lovingly over their son. Five seconds later she was dead.

'Go on.'

'Witnesses said I hit a parked car, and skidded sideways into a lorry travelling in the opposite direction.'

The young woman touched Brian's fingers again, but this time they lingered as he told her about the accident. She squeezed his hand gently as she got up from the table.

'I really am very sorry. But I have to go.'

Alex crept close to the hedge, stooping very slightly as she reached the entrance to the drive. She stood for a full minute watching the house, but all the windows were in darkness and she felt safe assuming that at three o'clock in the morning everyone would be in a deep sleep.

Slipping around the gatepost onto the lawn, careful not to crunch the gravel, she made her way to the garage door. Pushing a plastic card through the gap at the top, Alex jiggled it about with an experienced hand until the lock moved with a light click. She lifted the door very slowly, just enough so she had room to wriggle underneath, and switched on her head lamp. Moving carefully around the car, she tried the handle on the outhouse door. It wasn't locked.

Alex stepped inside and waited. Apart from the refrigerator humming quietly, there was no other sound. A faint smell of spices, disturbed by the light draught from outside, hung in the air. She walked softly along the hall, stopping to listen carefully when she reached the bottom of the stairs, and entered the lounge. Taking the watches from her pocket, she returned them to the sideboard, between the photographs of a young child and a beautiful woman with blonde hair and deep chestnut eyes.

Steamy Nights

'Green or black?' Julie called across the grassy patch outside the caravan door.

She was actually thinking *cyanide or arsenic.* And not for the first time in twenty odd years of marriage.

'She means red or white,' muttered her husband.

'Actually Will, I wouldn't mind a cuppa,' said Simon.

'Jules, that's one tea and a bottle of Shiraz. The tea's for Simon.'

Will turned back to the table.

'Still no sign of a job, Chris?' he asked.

'Christopher, my dear. No, nothing yet.'

'Huh,' huffed Will, eyes darting between tiles and board.

'Huh what?' asked Christopher.

'Not looking good,' said Will with a hearty laugh. 'Think I picked a duff lot here. Story of my life. Well, wife, actually.'

Simon glanced across the grass to see if Julie had heard.

'Ah, hang on. Here you go. S-E-X. Ten points. No extras, though. Bit like me and Julie. Never any extras. Nil points. You know, the nearest we've come to it latcly is when I chuck my boxers on top of her panties in the laundry basket. Bit different with you two from what I hear, unless you've just taken in a couple of stray dogs.

The walls between the flats are paper thin. Sometimes I wonder if they were built by Andrex.'

Julie plonked the wine bottle down next to Will.

'Sometimes I wonder we have any friends left,' she said sharply, 'and we'll be using separate laundry baskets from now on. Christopher's go.'

'OK,' said Christopher. 'I'll get straight to the point. C-R-U-X.'

'Right. What do we have here, then?' said Julie.

Scanning the last three turns, she picked four of her tiles to make the next word. G-R-E-E-N. She could feel Simon staring at her fingers as she placed the letters, and watched his face as she put down the final tile, deliberately slowly. He flared his nostrils as she counted her score, touching each of her fingertips, one at a time, to the top of her thumb. Julie had seen him do that before. Like a bull on heat.

Without any hesitation, Simon flicked Y-E-S onto the board. EYES. GREEN EYES.

'Simon's a sucker for green eyes,' said Christopher. 'He told me he's adored green eyes forever. Longer than he can remember.'

'Julie's got green eyes,' said Will. 'I've always thought they look a bit weird. Sort of imitation. You know what I mean?'

Julie stared at the words, her eyelids opening just a fraction wider for barely a second. The whistle from the kitchen broke an awkward silence.

'Come on, old girl, mash the tea.' Will leaned across the table and patted Julie on the head. 'We haven't got all night, and the salty air has made me thirsty as a fish on sand.'

Simon cleared his throat.

'Take your time, Julie,' he said softly. 'And I'll have green, if that's OK with you. Tea, that is.'

'Won't be long,' she said. 'Just keep playing along.'

Julie trod back across the dewy grass to the caravan. The kettle stopped whistling, the sound replaced by clinking crockery.

'Might just take a comfort break while Will's figuring out his word,' said Simon, stretching his arms towards the evening sky. 'Make room for the tea.'

Treading precisely in the marks left by her shoes, Simon followed Julie through the door. He had to push past her to get to the small toilet, and gently held her waist for a little longer than necessary as he squeezed behind. She was warm and relaxed, and couldn't help herself push towards him, just a little. Simon leaned forward slightly and brushed the back of her head with his lips. Her hair smelled of ripe avocado.

'Sorry, Simon. Can you manage?' Julie moved her arms and caught his hands, but he pressed them further into her soft waist, as though silently begging her to turn around.

'Bring some nibbles, Julie, I'm feeling a wee bit peckish,' Will shouted from outside.

Simon jumped and pulled his hands away.

'And talking of wee, is Simon still in the loo?'

Julie grunted at Will's crudeness. She squashed against the sink, allowing Simon just enough space to make his way to the toilet and poured boiling water into the teapot.

'He won't be long,' she answered, not particularly loudly since she could hear that Will hadn't bothered to wait for her reply.

'You two ever going to do one of those civil ceremonials, Chris?'

Will gave Christopher an exaggerated look straight between the eyes.

'Christopher, perlease, how many more times my dear. We've only been together a couple of years.'

'That's plenty long enough. Cripes, me and Julie were married in six months. Right little raver she was when we first got together. Couldn't leave me alone, know what I mean? Bit different now, for sure. You wouldn't believe...'

Julie banged the teapot down on the picnic table, the tiles scattering across the board.

'Would you mind not talking about me as though I wasn't here,' she said.

'Hells bells, you're touchy today. Scare the seagulls.'

Will shook his head slowly and began to rearrange the tiles.

Simon made a big show of checking the buttons on the front of his shorts as he made his way back to the table.

'What happened? I go for a wee and the game falls to pieces?'

'Will was just asking if we were planning anything connubial, but I told him I wasn't sure,' said Christopher.

He tried to catch Simon's eye, but his partner's gaze was firmly focussed on Julie.

'I said it might be a while,' he finished off.

Simon sat down and put his hands behind his head, pushing his legs forwards.

'Will, keep your feet to yourself, why don't you?' said Julie.

She glared across the table.

'Sorry,' said Simon, 'That was me. Just stretching.'

'Are you sure? Will has such immense feet.'

'You know what they say about blokes with big feet,' Will said. 'Not that you'd remember, Jules.'

Simon glanced sideways without moving his head. Julie's eyes glistened. His foot touched hers once again, gently this time.

'Right. Let's get this over and done with and off to bed,' said Julie, feeling another nudge, stronger. 'Whose go is it?'

'You know, I have such a lousy set of tiles here. Can't make out a single word.' Will knocked twice on the table. 'Chris, go for it, young man.'

'Any chance of a top-up?' Christopher pinged his empty glass.

Simon and Julie reached out for the Shiraz, grasping the bottle at the same time, their fingers wrapped around each other's. Simon took a deep breath.

'One of you will do,' laughed Christopher, holding out his glass. His eyes bored deeply into Simon's.

'You pour,' said Julie.

Simon gave a barely perceptible squeeze before she untwined her fingers. The tops of her ears felt hot, and she prayed they hadn't turned bright red.

'Yes, I can go,' said Christopher. 'C-H-I-L-L-I. Hope that's not too spicy for anyone.'

He raised his eyebrows, and looked over to Simon.

'Julie doesn't... ' Will was quick off the mark.

'...do spicy.'

Simon finished the sentence for him, nodding his head knowingly. 'Not much point in adding spice to old meat. Just makes it more unpalatable, don't you agree?'

Will wrinkled his brow, thought for a second or two, then gave a muted chuckle.

'Good one Simon, old chap.'

'Right, come on Julie, your turn.' Simon twitched a furtive wink across the corner of the table.

Julie's eyes scanned the board. She hadn't imagined it. Simon's KISS had followed her SOUL, his TOUCH followed her TENDER, and of course his EYES had appeared so quickly after her GREEN. Surely he must have been deliberately waiting for that.

Julie placed the last letter of her word.

S-T-E-A-M-Y.

She could feel Simon watching her fingers again as she positioned her tiles - no need to look at his face. The tip of her tongue protruded just a fraction between her lips. She wriggled uneasily in her chair and looked across at Will, who was talking enthusiastically to Christopher about how different his life could have been, if only this and if only that. Christopher's eyes were glazed, pointing in the general direction of the Shiraz he was twirling around the bottom of his glass, creating a hypnotic purple whirlpool.

Simon wiped the palms of his hands on his trousers.

Julie sensed his breathing becoming faster.

He rolled his tongue around his lips.

Julie probed his face for a clue.

Simon put down his word.

N-I-G-H-T-S.

Julie's lips moved as she said the words to herself. Now it was her turn to move her foot under the table so it rested lightly on one of Simon's legs. Simon stared hungrily at her beautiful green eyes.

STEAMY NIGHTS...

Modern Babylon

I coughed harder than ever before in all my thirty five years. Not daring to take another breath, I crashed the study door back on its hinges, dashed to the bathroom, and opened my mouth wide in front of the mirror. The toffee was jammed right at the back. Red faced and lungs at bursting point, I dislodged the sweet with a finger and spat it into the sink. Collapsing onto the toilet seat, I gulped air like someone rescued from drowning.

Jane shouted from downstairs.

'You OK, Pete?'

I stamped on the floor a couple of times. The stairs creaked, and the customary undisguised cursing about the threadbare carpet reached my ears a fraction of a second before my wife swept like a hurricane through the bathroom door.

'Heavens above, what on earth happened?'

Jane poured me a glass of water, and I took a few sips before finally letting my shoulders sag and leaning back onto the toilet cistern, still catching my breath.

'I thought at last the loose banister had taken its toll,' she said.

'Just checking my emails,' I hissed more than whispered. 'That guy down in Kent, the writer, bought a few books about London's West End, Covent Garden and all that?'

'Didn't he send you his biography?'

'Well, I just had an email from him with some bad news, took a sudden deep breath, and half swallowed a toffee. You heard the rest from downstairs. Take a look at what he said.'

I shuffled Jane into the study like a train engine, a 'just-married' thing we'd never grown out of. She peered at the computer screen through the bottom of her bifocals.

'Frederick Sage,' she said. 'Yes, I remember him.

'Start at the top, not the bottom,' I suggested.

Jane nodded slowly as she read through the email.

'Only two months to live... Get rid of my books... Would you like to buy them?'

Jane lowered herself slowly into the leather chair, and read the email for a second time.

'What a terrible shock for Fred and his family.' Jane pouted her ample lips, then perked up. 'What do you think? Would they be worth buying?'

'You mean you're wondering whether we can make a few quid from his bad luck.'

Sometimes I thought there was nothing Jane wouldn't do for money.

'No. Well, it wouldn't be like that. He asked.'

I knew exactly what was coming next.

'We badly need some extra cash for repairs to the house, so if you got them cheap...'

'We'd have to travel across to Maidstone, and that's a good couple of hours worrying if we'll get pulled over. No insurance, remember? I really don't know, Jane.'

Jane had a habit of twisting the long dangly strands of hair which fell across her face when she was losing patience. Her steel grey eyes dared me not to buy the books.

Reading the email again, I searched for a clue that there might be some hope of recovery for Fred, but his words painted a depressing finality, an irrevocable certainty that he wasn't long for this world.

'The idea of making a profit from someone dying gives me a very bad feeling.' A sinister shadow shivered through my body. 'As though something awful will happen.'

Looking through the study door at the rickety banister on the top landing, Jane twirled her hair faster than before.

'OK, OK. I'll drop him a note tomorrow morning with an offer for the job lot.'

I knew when to give in.

'Never realised Maidstone is such a big town,' Jane said, holding her forefinger on the map. She turned it around to match our direction of travel while at the same time keeping it faced towards the windscreen so there was some illumination from the street lamps.

'Turn right here, then left, and a couple of miles we're almost back on the main road.'

The meeting with Fred had been unexpectedly businesslike, but then my offer for the books wasn't particularly generous and he had more important things to think about than to haggle over the price. We'd packed the books, stacked them in the van and handed over the cash, all in less than half an hour.

The engine drone and rumble from the road was making me a little sleepy. I turned to ask Jane if she was feeling tired but she'd already dozed off, her head hanging to one side. She could still look cute. Sometimes.

Headlamps suddenly appeared from behind, and barely a moment later we were overtaken.

'What the hell was that?' I said. 'They must have been doing ninety, stupid beggars.'

No sooner had the car flashed past than I was blinded by two fiercely bright lights. I braked hard to the sound of rubber squealing on tarmac, and swung the van to the left, stopping just short of a collision. Jane woke up with a yell and threw her arms forward, her frightened face lit up by the spot lamps then only a couple of feet in front of the bonnet.

'Lock the doors, Pete. Lock the bloody doors. Now!'

Jane couldn't disguise the quiver in her voice as two burly figures, dressed in dark overalls and with balaclavas, made towards the van. I hit the button on the door, and the locks clicked just as the first to arrive pulled on the driver's side handle.

'Open up. We won't hurt you.'

The fixed stare and the urgency of his voice indicated he meant business.

'Hold on, Jane,' I grunted, crunching the gearbox into reverse.

'Pete!' Jane screamed.

I whipped my head sideways to see a gun pointing at the passenger window. My foot slipped from the pedal, the van jerked backwards a few inches and the engine stalled.

'Hey, just unlock the doors will you,' one of them shouted through the windscreen. 'We'll do what we came for and be on our way.'

He stood up, but I couldn't catch what he said to his accomplice.

We watched as they walked past, and Jane realised just before I did.

'The back doors, Pete. They can get in the back.'

The rear of the van flew open.

'Just sit there, look to the front and don't move a muscle,' bellowed the first man. I turned around and instantly wished I hadn't.

Crack! The sound deafened my ears, and a white flash lit up the inside of the van as part of the centre console shattered into a million fragments. Jane drew her legs up to her body, grabbed her knees, and gave a high pitched squeal.

'Pete, just leave it,' she shrieked, but I didn't need to be told.

We sat motionless as the men ran to and from their car with the bags of books. One, two, nothing to do but count, eight, then nine trips. They jumped in their car, switched off the spot lamps, and drove off into the darkness, their number plate veiled in a cloud of dust.

Hardly daring to move, I held out a hand to Jane, and found she was shivering even though the night air was balmy. Squeezing her arm for reassurance, mine more than hers, I unlocked the driver's door and stepped outside into the eerie dark silence. The lingering smell of scorched rubber reminded me that this was more than a bad dream, not a nightmare I could simply wake up from to be forgotten over a cup of tea.

Stumbling on the uneven verge, I walked awkwardly to the back of the van and peered inside. All the books had gone. I shrugged my shoulders, wide-eyed yet composed. Quietly closing the rear doors, I slumped back into the driver's seat, looking straight ahead, hardly breathing.

'Come on, Pete. They've gone.' Jane tugged my arm. 'You said something awful might happen, and it did. That's it. Home.'

I took a deep breath, gave Jane a weak smile, and started the engine.

'What a mess,' Jane shouted above the noise of the vacuum cleaner as she set to work in the front of the van. 'Bits of plastic everywhere, even here under the seat.'

I looked through from the back when I heard the whine subside. Jane was struggling to reach between the passenger and driver's seats.

'Can't quite get it, hang on, that's it.' She held up an old book. 'Must have been thrown forwards when you had to brake so quickly last night.'

Jane joined me at the rear of the van.

'Well, we still have one of the books, it seems. *Unsentimental Journeys through Modern Babylon.* Greenwood.'

I took the book and flicked through to the title page. Head, Hole & Co., Ivy Lane, Paternoster Row, and Farringdon Street, E.C., 1867. Between the publisher and the book title, an inscription, in faded black, scratchy in places where the ink was missing:

'To Mother Dearest, James, August 1867,' Jane read it out loud.

'James Greenwood. He wrote about London life in the mid 19th century,'

'So it's signed by the author just after publication, must be a first edition then, probably worth quite a bit.'

I instinctively hid the book inside my jacket as a car drove past, my mind switching between excitement and trepidation so quickly it made me slightly breathless. Locking the van, we carried the book up to the study for a closer look.

'The illustrations are fabulous, all in pen and ink,' said Jane as she turned the pages.

'This one of the London Horse Market is wonderful, and look at this, Mr Dodd's Dust-Yard. Those poor women with sieves. What on earth can they be looking for?'

The shrill ring from the office phone brought me back from Victorian London with a start. My hand hovered above the receiver and I raised my eyebrows as I turned to Jane.

'Well, go on Pete, pick it up. It's not going to be James Greenwood, is it?'

I raised the handset slowly to my ear.

'Hello.'

'Hello, is that Peter? Frederick here. You came over last night to pick up some books.'

'Oh, good morning Fred. Is everything alright?'

I exhaled softly through pursed lips. That was it then. I was certain Fred was calling to say he had accidentally let us take one of his more valuable books.

'Yes, thank you. Except the obvious, of course. But a strange thing happened just after you drove off. A couple of chaps were asking about a book. Said they'd seen it on a list I put up in the library, before I thought of asking if you wanted them. Anyway, I told them the whole lot had just gone. One of the chaps was pulling his collar away from his neck, his face quite red, flustered he was. I said that if the book was that important, you would probably let them have it, and described your van in case they could catch you up. It was, oh, barely fifteen minutes since you'd left.'

'Fred...'

'I really didn't think it would do any harm, but then over breakfast I started to wonder...'

'Fred, Fred, hang on, listen to me. This is very important.' I stopped him in mid-sentence.

'Did you give them our address?' I asked him, suddenly clammy with a new fear.

'Only your email. I have no idea where you live exactly, somewhere near Gatwick, isn't it?'

'OK, thanks Fred.' My heart slowed a little, although I could still feel it pounding, and a bead of nervous perspiration fell onto my cheek. 'Did you know there was a signed James Greenwood first edition in the heap of books?'

Jane opened her eyes as wide as circles, her mouth falling open.

'Why are you telling him that?' she whispered.

I covered the mouthpiece.

'The poor guy is dying, and has no idea he just sold a book worth possibly thousands for less than a quid.'

'Peter, I just bought the books for research. Will never get to finish my latest one now and I'm no longer in the slightest bit interested in books, money or anything much else if it comes to that. If you can get a good price for the book, you're welcome to it. At least you'll talk about me to your friends and family long after I've gone.'

Fred blew his nose, and after a few seconds silence the phone crackled and went dead. I replaced the receiver gently, pulled out a handkerchief and wiped my brow.

Jane held her head in both hands.

'Pete? What did he say?'

'We can keep the book. But do you think we should?'

I was still chilled by the thought that those guys had a gun, and clearly weren't afraid to use it to get what they wanted.

'OK, the book's not going to give us what we've always dreamed of, Pete. But it could help us pay for a few repairs. No more creaky stairs, dodgy banisters, or leaking windows.'

'I really don't know,' I shook my head slowly, looking Jane in the eye. 'A drink. That's what we need.'

Jane opened the filing drawer where I kept my Johnnie Walker and pulled it out together with two tumblers. She poured us both more than she ought to have done.

Taking a glass from her, I sank into my old leather chair and took a lengthy sip, the earthy taste spreading warmly across my tongue. The alcohol found its way to my brain within seconds, and for the first time since the ambush I began to relax.

Jane sat on the edge of the desk turning the pages of the book.

'We might even be able to afford a proper shower, and... '

I caught her eye again.

'What?' she asked. 'Why are looking at me like that?'

'No. The book has got to go. Think about it Jane. Those thugs could have killed us last night. They have my email address, and I'd like to bet they can hit on a way of finding out where we live. It's not worth the risk.'

Jane put on my favourite smile, the one that almost always got her what she wanted. Catching up with what I'd just said, the smile faded.

'But how will they know we haven't got it? They'll still be around once they find the address.'

I'd already thought that through.

'We'll take it up to Bloomsbury Auctions this afternoon, and leave it with them. They'll have a good idea what it's worth, and it shouldn't be long before their next sale.'

'But the thugs will still think we've got the book, so we might as well get some benefit from it.'

I checked the directory, picked up the phone and dialled the Crawley Gazette.

'Hello. I have a front page story for you.'

'Don't do this, Pete. You'll be sorry.'

'We have to let those guys know we no longer have the book.'

'But there has to be another way Pete,' said Jane. 'We so need that money. I'm telling you now, you will be very sorry if you do this. Think of the repairs that need doing.'

'This is more important than a rickety banister,' I said. 'We could be dead if they catch up with us.'

Jane tried to grab the phone but I pushed her away and glared angrily at her for the first time I could remember.

'Yes, I'm still here. This is it. Local couple plan to donate proceeds from sale of valuable antiquarian book...'

Jane banged her glass down onto the desk, and a plume of whisky splashed over the top. She stomped out of the study. Stopping at the door, she looked back, shaking her head furiously.

'Fine,' she spat. 'I'll be downstairs.'

Catching her foot in a carpet thread, Jane tripped forwards onto the loose banister. It broke away from the wall with a loud snap.

Chocolate Surprise

Her eyes snapped shut as Wendy rubbed them with the back of her hand. Tears squeezed through the lids and flooded down her face, drawing charcoal black trails of mascara. She reached across the sink, waved her arms about to find the cold tap, rinsed her hands and splashed cold water on her face.

Removing the damp towel pressed over her eyes, she heaved a sigh as a beam of light flicked across the kitchen wall.

'And there was me trying to get ahead before the guests arrive.'

A car door slammed.

Dabbing her cheeks with a clean handkerchief, Wendy just had time to check her face in the hall mirror before the doorbell chimed. She creaked open the door, bloodshot eyes peering around the edge.

'Wendy?'

'Mr Wagstaffe! I'd recognise you anywhere, even after all these tears. Years. Do come in. You're the first to turn up.'

Mr Wagstaffe stamped snow from his sandals, and strutted into the hall, hastily regaining his balance after one foot slipped on the polished tiles. Bushy eyebrows sprouted forwards at least an inch from his forehead, which went on forever, his grey crinkly hair forming a perfect horseshoe at the back. The baggy blue suit, green shirt and orange tie were too much for Wendy, who spluttered a laugh even louder than the mismatched attire.

Mr Wagstaffe raised just one of his eyebrows, which brought Wendy down with a jolt. That was exactly how she remembered him from the sixth form. 'Wendy,' he would say. 'If you were using an abacus you'd lose the beads.' Or 'My dear girl, if Pythagoras could hear you he would doubt his own theorem.' Or something else to make her hang her head in front of her friends.

'Sorry, Mr Wagstaffe, I think I might have started too early on the wine.'

Wendy wiped away more tears with her mascara-stained handkerchief.

'I'll get you a glass,' she said as she returned to the kitchen.

Wendy chopped the last of the chillies ready for the soup she'd prepared earlier. She didn't usually add chillies to her soups, and if she did it was rarely red chillies, and if it was it was never Scotch Bonnet. Until today, that is. Maybe. One moment she hovered the chopping board over the soup ready to brush in the chillies, and the next she lay it back on the worktop, not sure whether to add them or not.

Ding dong. The doorbell added some urgency to the decision. She picked up the chopping board and, hesitating for the last time, swept the chopped chillies into the soup.

Hurriedly pouring Mr Wagstaffe's glass of *Gluhwein*, Wendy handed it over as she passed him in the living room on the way to answer the door.

'Ross, how lovely of you to come. It must be what, five years?'

'Wendy, you're looking great. But then you always did.'

Dropping Ross off at the living room, and making a couple of quick introductory remarks, Wendy left him with Mr Wagstaffe and hurried back to the kitchen to make sure her dessert was in order.

'Well, er Ron, how did you come to know Wendy?'

Mr Wagstaffe peered closely at a painting on the living room wall.

'Actually, it's Ross.'

'So, how did you and Wendy meet?'

'Oh, in a shop. I was with my girlfriend while she was buying a new dress, and Wendy served us. While I was waiting outside the fitting room, I couldn't take my eyes off her. So I slipped a business card into her hand as I paid. We got together a few weeks later and within six months we were engaged to be married.'

Mr Wagstaffe was trying to read the signature on the painting. 'Hmm. Must be a copy. So what happened?'

'One day I was out with Wendy looking at shoes, and the girl in the shop was an absolute stunner. So I slipped a business card into her hand as I paid, but Wendy saw what I'd done. She hung her head, took off her ring and placed it gently on the counter. That was me dumped, there and then, in the shop, in front of everyone. How heartless can you get?'

Mr Wagstaffe raised an eyebrow.

'And are you settled with anyone now?'

'No. For some reason, nothing seems to work out.'

The lengthy silence that followed was broken only by the whir of an electric mixer in the kitchen. Wendy looked at the dessert with a smile of satisfaction on her lips. Rich Chocolate Mousse with a Twist. Two large bars of strong dark chocolate, three eggs, and an extra special ingredient which had been in and out of the medicine cabinet so many times that Wendy had lost count.

'Was that the door again?' shouted Mr Wagstaffe.

It was too late to be having second thoughts she decided, and that would be her final dinner guest.

'Oh, Mrs Leary, you managed to find the house.'

'Yes, my dear, no trouble at all. Just got held up a bit at the shop. Someone wanted to complain about a dress. You remember how it is, to be sure.'

It was Wendy's first job after leaving school, and initially it was fabulous. She enjoyed it no end. Except it did end. With Mrs Leary. 'Wendy, there's a mistake in the stock book.' Or, 'Wendy, you must have short-changed this customer.' Or, 'Wendy, the sizes aren't in order on that rail.' Over the following weeks, Wendy's shoulders drooped lower, her smile disappeared and her once-sprightly step turned to a shuffle.

Taking Mrs Leary's coat and guiding her through to the living room, she thrust a glass of mulled wine into her hand as she introduced her to the others.

'Do excuse me for a bit while I put the main course in the oven. Chatter amongst yourselves.'

Wendy carried on through to the kitchen.

'Well, this should be an enjoyable evening,' started Mr Wagstaffe. 'Such a lovely idea of Wendy's to have a get-together like this. Don't know about you two, but I'm quite taken aback that she even remembers me.'

Mrs Leary looked down at Mr Wagstaffe's sandals.

'Well, difficult to forget from what I'm looking at,' she said. 'Pleased to meet you. Both. Have you known Wendy long?'

'As it happens, I haven't seen her since she left school seven or eight years back,' said Mr Wagstaffe. 'Left with no qualifications. Went into some dead end shop girl job, I think. And you?'

'As it happens,' Mrs Leary pushed her lips forward and slowly raised her eyes, taking in Mr Wagstaffe's suit on her way up. 'As it *happens*, Wendy was one of *my* shop girls.'

'Take a seat everyone, dinner's almost ready,' Wendy called from the kitchen.

Mr Wagstaffe was careful not to sit next to Mrs Leary.

Wendy put on her very best angelic smile as she served the soup.

'I've added a little something to spice up the starter.'

'Should be fine Wendy,' said Mrs Leary sniffing the air. 'Soup can often be quite boring, don't you think?'

Mr Wagstaffe looked suspiciously at his bowl.

'What are those little red bits?'

Before Wendy could say 'Scotch Bonnet', Mrs Leary had taken a spoonful. Her eyes opened so wide her eyeballs looked in danger of falling out.

At the same time, Ross dipped some fresh bread into his soup and popped it in his mouth just as Mr Wagstaffe's left eyebrow shot up, and beads of sweat joined together to form a lagoon on his bald crown. With his horseshoe of hair, the top of his head looked like a map of a coral island. With real water.

'Am I on fire, or what?' said Ross, grinning as he went for a second dip. 'Wow, Wendy, this sure has a kick!'

Just wait until it hurries its way out, thought Wendy as she smiled an acknowledgement.

Mrs Leary's eyes were running freely by the time she'd managed half her soup.

'Please could I have a glass of water, my dear?'

Wendy cleared her bowl from the table, having carefully just skimmed the surface of the soup as she pretended to dip her bread, and returned from the kitchen with a jug of iced water and three glasses.

'There you go. Sorry if I over-did the spices a bit. Do excuse me while I sort out our main course.'

Wendy disappeared into the kitchen.

'You know, she never was very dependable, that girl,' whispered Mrs Leary, leaning across the table, 'She probably put too much spice in because she used tablespoons instead of teaspoons.'

Mr Wagstaffe, his eyebrow not quite back to normal from the chillies, nodded slowly, staring at the large quantity of soup he had left in his bowl.

'I know, I know. Mathematics was definitely not Wendy's best subject at school. She could add two and two and get five. Always having to pull her up, I was. Gave the other kids a good laugh, though.'

'Nope, not the smartest owl in the tree,' agreed Ross. 'Didn't take me long to find someone far more interlectoral.

'Intellectual,' muttered Mr Wagstaffe.

'Mind you,' said Mrs Leary as she wiped chilli tears from her eyes for the umpteenth time. 'She can't be all bad, can she? Invited us to this little get-together after all, she did.'

Ross made a clatter with his soup spoon.

'Shush, she's coming.'

Wendy had balanced two large oval dinner plates on each arm.

'Well guys, here's the main course. The Yorkshire has risen nicely. Hope you all like Toad in the Hole.'

Under her breath, she added 'Very appropriate.'

Wendy slid what was indeed an ample plateful in front of each of her three guests.

'Them there three sausages are on the big size, Wendy,' said Mrs Leary, not sure whether she was seeing straight as her eyes were still blushed from the soup.

'Yes, they're handmade, from the butcher's. Don't want you going home feeling hungry,' replied Wendy.

'So thoughtful,' said Mrs Leary.

Raising his customary eyebrow, Mr Wagstaffe opened his mouth to ask Wendy whether she would mind if he only ate two sausages, when the hostess returned to the kitchen to emerge with a large tray of dishes containing Brussels sprouts, roasted potatoes and a huge jug of gravy.

'There you go. How about that for a reunion feast?'

Still on a high after the chillies in the soup, Ross added a heap of the beautifully browned and crispy potatoes and a pyramid of sprouts to his plate.

'This looks fabulous, Wendy.'

Wendy put her head on one side, taking a long look at her former fiancé.

'Just wondering how we would have turned out if you hadn't been a serial love rat.'

Ross decided she was just kidding and pulled a wide grin. Wendy responded with one of her own. *He had no idea, poor thing.*

Mrs Leary turned up the corner of her lip.

'Just a few sprouts then dear, since there's not many left.'

'Have as many as you like,' said Wendy. 'There's plenty more out the back.'

Mr Wagstaffe was the last to clear his plate, and leaned back with one hand pressing each side of his ample stomach.

'Right, didn't you say there was chocolate mousse for dessert?' he asked, blowing out his cheeks. 'I shall have to be going soon.'

'You certainly will,' said Wendy.

Mrs Leary, who had been reading the label on the wine bottle looked up. 'Yes, let's see if it's as good as you say.'

Wendy's smile flattened. She didn't move a muscle. Not a twitch. All of a sudden the extra special ingredient in the mousse seemed a bad idea. Revenge is not always sweet, she thought.

'I'm not sure it has quite set,' was the best Wendy could manage. Her tongue crept out between her lips, and her eyes opened wide to perfect circles.

'Go on Wendy, we really want to try it,' challenged Mrs Leary, keen to pour scorn on the sloppy dessert. 'Are they in the fridge?'

She shot up from the table, faster than she'd moved all evening.

Before Wendy could stop her, Mrs Leary marched into the kitchen and returned with the mousses balanced precariously on a tray.

Wendy vigorously shook her head, her tongue plopped back inside and the glaze over her eyes vanished.

'No, you can't. I mean you can't eat it. I mean you can't. Possibly. Eat it. Yet.'

She threw her leg out as Mrs Leary walked past the end of the table. Mrs Leary tripped, Wendy lost her balance and tumbled off her chair. The tray flew clean over Mr Wagstaffe's head, the four mousses making a surprisingly symmetrical pattern as they slid down the wall behind him.

'That was close,' said Mr Wagstaffe, lifting his eyebrow.

Mrs Leary threw her arms around Ross' neck to steady herself and landed on his lap. Ross made the sound of a deflating balloon, and the second he could take a breath, helped her off.

Wendy was sprawled face down on the floor, her bottom bobbing in time with her sobs. She twisted onto her back, tears of laughter running down her face.

'You have no idea how close,' she laughed.

Ross was the first to speak, 'You OK, Wendy?'

'Yes, thank you. I'm feeling so much better. A perfect end to the evening.'

The Lift

The aroma from the coffee shop is enticing, but my feet are hot and throbbing and my arms I swear are an inch longer than when setting out for the shops. And I'm late. Not only late, I'm *late*, and suddenly there are baby buggies and little kiddies everywhere I look.

Quickening my pace, I resist the temptation of a caffeine fix and march past the coffee shop. Flicking my thick black hair forwards so the counter is hidden from view, I press the knob to summon the lift to the car park instead. Quite a crowd assembles behind me and I just have time to jab the button for the fourth floor before they pile in and squeeze me to the back. Not for the first time in my twenty years I wish I'd turned out a bit taller.

Peering down through the glass wall at the rear of the lift I can see baristas pressing coffee grounds, steaming milk and serving up foamed cappuccinos. The ping when we arrive at the second floor rings in good news because the lift empties and I get to make the final two floors alone. Picking up my bags I spot an envelope on the floor. It looks well trodden-on, but with child-like fascination I stoop and pick it up. Was it there when I got in the lift? I'm not sure. Somebody could have just that minute dropped it.

I rush to the car and toss the shopping bags unceremoniously into the boot, then dash back to the lift and make my way to the second floor just in case anyone is looking around for a lost letter. Apart from a young child, who has discovered that if he yells loudly enough his voice ricochets around the almost-empty car park, and his parents, clearly suffering from selective deafness, there is no-one to be seen.

The alluring smell of hot coffee and toasted Panini wafting up from below at last gets the better of me, so free from shopping bags I make my way back to the lift and press for the ground floor.

'Large cappo, double shot, cream and mallows, please'.

'Need a bit of a boost, then.' It wasn't so much a question. The barista grinned as he squirted whipped cream onto the coffee. 'Extra mallows should put a smile on your face. Hello?'

'Oh, sorry, yes, thanks. It's been a long one.' I want to tell him, anyone, that I'm *late* but there's someone else who should know first.

Picking out a soft leather sofa at the edge of the coffee shop, I flop down close to where a young, goatee-bearded chap in black tails and white bow tie is promoting copies of his CD by playing Chopin on electric cello.

The lift and the coffee shop share centre stage in the shopping arcade, the tables arranged open plan with a low glass partition where the shoppers pass by. A regular source of amusement to me is to contemplate which of them will walk past the lift and who will next be seen whooshing their way to the car park floors above.

The soft leather, the paradoxical taste of sweet marshmallow, rich fresh cream and bitter Italian caffè, blend to shift me into neutral. That chap with the determined expression has his keys out. A dead cert for the lift.

Making an abrupt change of style to Classical Gas, the cellist startles me out of my little guessing game. Kicking off my shoes and folding my legs underneath my bottom, curiosity gets the better of me and I reach for the envelope and examine it more closely. Slowly turning it around, the grubby smudges give nothing away. I pull around the flap carefully to try to make it look as though it has never been opened, and grunt when the paper rips.

There is, indeed, a letter inside. OK, I shouldn't read it, but hey, I'm *late*, so some emotional slack is surely allowed.

'*Dear Lucy,*' Lucy? My toes curl under without me telling them to.

'*Dear Lucy,*' The handwriting is familiar. I am so not ready for this.

'*Dear...*' The edges of the letter quiver in time with my quickening heartbeat.

'*...Lucy,*' My hands are like icicles yet sweaty. I can sense colour draining from my face. There is no need for me to read further. Jack had told me he didn't want children too soon. And I'm *late*. He had somehow guessed.

My hands are trembling, I am so cold I shiver, my lips are pressed tightly closed between my teeth, salt from my tears creeping inside. I could do with more coffee, but I'm too fragile to move and just stare at the words on the paper until they drift out of focus and I fall into an abstract trance. The notes from the cello mingle with the noise of the crowds into an omelette of meaningless clamour.

Gradually lifting my gaze, teary eyes still in soft focus, my fuddled brain makes out a familiar image hurrying past the coffee shop towards the lift. I jump up, catching the table with my knee and sending the cold coffee flying to the floor. At first my legs won't work and I stumble into the couple seated next to me. Although my mouth moves with the words, no apology comes out. I try again to walk, and this time make it out into the mall. Each step brings me closer to reality, and by the time I reach the lift my senses have mostly returned.

Pressing the button before they completely close, the doors glide open with the anticipation of stage curtains on opening night. Jack seems to recognise the letter in my hand an instant before he realises it is me holding it, and shakes his head slowly. His eyes lock on to mine.

'Lucy, give me the letter.'

Haunted Dreams

I squeezed my size five feet into the size four shoes that Bob had bought me for my birthday. Men!

'Hurry up, or Sue and Steve will get to the restaurant before us.'

'I'll only be a couple of minutes,' Bob shouted down the stairs.

The youngest of the four of us, I was the last to reach forty, which seemed a good thing. But at the same time I was rather sorry that the milestone was being celebrated with so much fuss. A quiet night in with Bob would have been less stressful. Still, it was too late to worry about that now.

'You look wonderful in that dress,' said Bob as he walked down the stairs, his eyes twinkling like they did when he really meant what he said.

'You scrub up pretty well yourself for a wrinkly!'

Bob was only two years older, but he had that mature look about him which often makes middle aged men so attractive. You know what I mean?

We had driven to the New George once or twice a week for the past ten years since the old traditional pub had been knocked down and replaced by a more modern affair with a splendid restaurant. There had been a petition raised in the village to stop it being demolished but the brewery argued it was modernisation or closure.

Some of the locals had taken their custom elsewhere, but the pub was now more popular than it had ever been in recent times. And judging by the number of cars, today was no exception.

'I told you they'd be here before us', I sighed, spotting Steve's car as we pulled off the road into the car park, crunching across the loose flints. Bob reversed into the adjoining space while I teased my hair in the vanity mirror. I needed a change so had let it grow longer, almost touching my shoulders. Friends said I looked younger.

'Do you think this colour suits me, or is it too young?'

'Your hair looks fine. I love mouse.'

I reached across to put my hands around Bob's throat, but he was too quick and jumped out of the car.

'Come on Bren, we'll be late!'

'Hi Brenda. Hi Bob.'

Sue waved as we walked into the lounge bar.

'What are you having to drink, Birthday Girl?' said Steve, getting up and giving me a hug as we reached their table.

I was seriously in the mood for a gin and tonic, but Bob had to make do with a half pint of bitter. There was no way I was going to drive us home tonight.

Sue wanted to know what Bob had bought me for my fortieth, how it felt to be as old as the rest of them, why I'd chosen this particular tint for my hair, and where I'd gone to have my nails done to match. Steve and Bob gave up trying to swing the conversation, and do you know they eventually yawned. Bob somehow managed to combine his with a splutter of laughter, and if you've ever heard that tried before you'll know why we all joined in.

'Why don't we find a table and order dinner?' I said. 'All this avoiding talk about engines, planes and golf has made me hungry.'

As it happens, my motive was not just hunger. I had been watching people come and go from the other end of the pub where the food tables were, and had noticed a waiter who seemed a little out of place. No, he wasn't handsome, or young, or tall, or have any kind of wow factor. I couldn't put a finger on it, but there was something familiar about him. You get that feeling sometimes?

'Let's go for that table by the window,' I said, a feeling of anticipation paddling around my tummy.

The waiter, that waiter, took our orders. Although talking to the others, I was pretty sure he spent longer than necessary looking at me. And I was definitely the one on the receiving end of his smile as he flipped closed his order pad and walked to the kitchen. I couldn't help but watch him all the way.

'Looks like you have an admirer,' said Bob.

'Flattery at forty is not a bad thing,' Sue said with a bit of a giggle.

Ah, yes, flattery. That's what it was. Someone must have told the waiter about my birthday. I breathed a sigh of relief as I kicked off my new high heels under the table.

'No frowning on your birthday please!' said Bob, and I confess I jumped a little. In my mind I was somewhere else, miles away, years back. I knew that waiter.

'You OK Brenda?' asked Sue.

I nodded, but was lost for the right words and we sat silently waiting for our meal to be served.

'Thanks Tom,' said Brenda as the waiter leaned across with her grilled trout.

'Where do you know him from, Bren?' asked Sue. 'I don't remember having seen him here before.'

'Me neither,' Brenda replied.

'But you called him 'Tom'!' laughed Bob.

'Well, I'm sure I didn't,' Brenda insisted. 'Let's just get on and enjoy our meal, shall we?'

I tried not to sound flustered, but didn't pull it off. Sue and Steve gave each other one of those wide-eyed glances that says don't mess with this, and Bob stared at his plate.

'Sorry,' I said, stretching the last syllable and turning it into the best grin I could muster. Sue reached across and squeezed my hand like you would a little kid who had unwillingly owned up to stealing a first kiss.

I looked around the restaurant but there must have been a change of shift. I couldn't see my waiter. My waiter? Must have had a gin too many. Tom. I said his name over and over in my head. Tom, Tom, Tom. Even as we were driving home. Tom. He was my last thought as I fell to sleep.

A blinding burst of light woke me with a start. My legs kicked out like I was running for my life.

'What's the matter, Brenda?' said a distant voice, then closer. 'Brenda?'

I was staring at the ceiling, my eyes frantically trying to focus, when suddenly I jerked upright.

'Tom,' I said, catching my breath between sobs of sadness. 'It's Tom, the waiter. At the pub. Tom.'

I told Bob about the dream. The same dream, night after night. The air-raid siren going off incessantly, how the war was getting Tom down, how he had lost his temper and started up foolish arguments over nothing that really mattered. And his accusation that his wife was constantly nagging. I could see her hands gently stroking her belly and hear her pleading even now.

'No, Tom, please don't go yet. I need to tell you about something important.'

Tom pulled himself up and marched towards the sitting room door. He made a point of not looking back as he swung it open and stepped outside.

'Tom, please. We have to talk.'

A torrent of scorching air smacked into his back as the bomb exploded through the roof of the house.

Tears ran down my face as I turned to Bob.

'His wife was killed. With the child he never saw.'

'What do you mean, he isn't here?'

The landlord at the George said the waiter had arrived out of the blue the day before looking for casual work. But today, although he had been due to start at eleven, he hadn't turned up.

We ordered drinks and sat at the bar watching the entrance, but Tom didn't appear.

'Come on, one o'clock. Let's go Bren,' said Bob. 'He's not going to come this late in the day.'

We drove reluctantly out of the car park and headed for home. I was feeling a little sleepy, probably because of the restless night and the lunchtime drink, and began to doze. My head lolled to one side as we rounded a sharp bend in the road, and I opened my eyes just in time to see someone directly ahead of the car. I screamed.

'Bob!'

Bob had already seen him, and slammed his foot hard on the brake pedal. The tyres screeched as the wheels locked in a split second, but we were too close to have any chance of stopping. The man made no attempt to dodge out of the way. He opened his mouth, but I couldn't hear what he was saying. Barely three seconds had passed since I had yelled out, but it seemed a lifetime. Everything was happening in slow motion.

The car stopped, slewed into the hedge at a dizzy angle. There had been no bump. No crashing of glass. No sickening thud as we hit the man. Nothing except the strong smell of smouldering rubber from the tyres.

Bob switched off the ignition, and looked across at me.

'Did we hit him?' I asked, my voice shaking a little.

'We must have done. I don't see how we could have missed. He was right in front of the car as we went round the bend. There was no time to do anything.'

'You go and look.'

Bob turned around in his seat. The man was lying in the middle of the road.

'Bren. Bren! He looks like the waiter. It's your Tom!'

I can't remember who was out of the car first, but we ran back, fearing the very worst.

Tom's eyes locked onto mine as I knelt down beside him.

'There was no time to say good-bye before...'

'Before when?' I asked him, knowing full well what he was going to say.

'The bomb,' he replied. 'I left you behind. I'm sorry.'

'What does all this mean, Bob?' I turned away from Tom. 'He knows exactly what happens in my dream.'

A cold shiver tickled my spine, and when I looked back there was nothing there except an empty road. No body. No blood stains. Nothing to suggest the terrible accident that had occurred only minutes earlier.

'Bob,' I whispered. 'Where has he gone?

Bob walked slowly back to the spot where Tom had been, and stared at the grey tarmac.

'Well, he certainly isn't here.'

At least, he wasn't anywhere to be seen.

The Blue Suit

'Would you have time to take my blue suit into the cleaners?' Rupert said as he wiped up some egg from his plate with a piece of bread.

'No problem,' I replied, juggling a slice of hot toast between my hands. 'Is there anything else you need in town while I'm there?'

I was going to make a morning of it with Jane. She and Martin had lived next door for some time, and we were good friends.

Rupert washed his breakfast down with a final gulp of strong black coffee, stood up from the table, and slipped his jacket over broad shoulders.

'I might be a bit late from the office tonight. The boss has someone coming in and he wants me to join them for drinks after work.'

'That's OK. I won't start dinner until later.'

'Maybe best give dinner a miss altogether,' he said. 'You know how these things can go on.'

I was used to these business meetings, but didn't much enjoy eating alone. I usually ended up making a quick sandwich and eating it in front of the television. Still, at least we had a lovely house and didn't want for anything.

Rupert picked up his phone and briefcase from the kitchen table and gave me a quick peck on the cheek as he breezed out of the front door and slammed it shut. Giving him just enough time to start the car and reverse down the drive, I opened the door and waved from the porch as he drove off. It had been years since Rupert had bothered to wave back, but that didn't stop me going through the same routine each morning. Out of the corner of my eye, I thought I caught a glimpse of Jane at the window next door but if I had, she was gone when I turned my head to smile in her direction.

'Blue suit,' I said out loud, and caught a crumb of toast from the corner of my mouth with my tongue as I started up the stairs.

Opening Rupert's wardrobe, I shuffled through the clothes hanging on the rail and lifted out the blue suit. Laying it on the bed, I pulled a handkerchief from one of the trouser pockets, and rolled them up into a neat bundle. Rupert was usually careful not to leave anything in his suit jackets, but I reckoned the first time I didn't check would be the time he had left something important inside.

'I knew it!' I said, laughing as I threw an envelope from the inside pocket on to the bed. The breast pocket revealed a couple of theatre tickets which I was sure must have been old as we hadn't been to see a show for months.

I took a quick look at the tickets, and didn't recognise the name of the production. And the date was recent, last Thursday in fact. But we hadn't been out last Thursday. Anyway, Rupert had to stay over in the city that night because he had a meeting with a client and hadn't been able to make it home. My tummy did a flip.

I picked up the envelope and sat on the edge of the bed. In the top left hand corner, in small capital letters, was written 'JANE'. I turned it over and over, feeling my breathing getting heavier each time. Taking an extra deep breath I dared to open the flap. The envelope was empty. Nothing in it.

Slowly, small suspicions which I had thrown to the wind over the last few months returned, one by one. The times Rupert was supposed to be working late at the office, but wasn't there when I phoned. When I was so sure I had seen his car in town, but he'd said he hadn't been anywhere near there that day. When he had spent a whole week totally distracted by something on his mind, which he had said were problems with a new project at work.

The phone on Rupert's bedside table rang and jolted my train of thought. I shook my head to clear it a little and picked up.

'Jane. Oh, hello Jane.' I tried very hard not to sound upset.

'How'd you and Rupert like to pop round this evening for drinks. There's something I need to talk to you about.'

At least he wasn't seeing her tonight, then.

'Sue... Sue, are you there?'

I swallowed hard.

'You want to talk? Is it important?'

I knew my voice was a bit shaky, but managed to control it quite well, all things considered.

'Yes, it is, quite.' Jane sounded so cool.

I wanted a chance to talk to Rupert before meeting with Jane head on.

'Can't it wait 'til the weekend? We're a bit busy for the next few evenings.'

'Well, I suppose it could, but it's really important, and affects all of us. I'd much rather you could make it tonight.'

Jane's tone had hardened noticeably, like someone who was not going to give up until she got her way.

'Shall we say eight?'

It would be tight, but hopefully I would have time to quiz Rupert before then.

'OK, Jane, if you insist. See you about eight o'clock.'

I replaced the receiver, and sat staring at the wall, trying to make sense of what was going on. Rupert and *Jane*? Jane next door? OK, there had been a few bad times, but Jane? Her best friend?

Suddenly I remembered that Rupert was going to be late home that evening, because of the meeting with the boss.

'That's if there is any such meeting,' I spat the words out loud. 'Rupert, how could you do this to me? I shall never, ever forgive you. How could you *do* it!'

Grabbing the blue suit from the bed, I pulled the jacket from the hanger and tore the breast pocket. Surprised at my own strength, I ripped the rest of the suit into shreds. If the doorbell hadn't rung, the whole wardrobe would have been in danger of destruction.

I looked down to the front porch, and shuddered when I recognised the top of Jane's head. Bundling the pieces in my arms, I ran downstairs and pulled open the front door so quickly I could see I'd made Jane jump with surprise.

'Sue, I hope you don't mind, but....' my ex-best friend stopped in mid-sentence. 'What on earth's the matter? What have you done to your lovely nails?'

Looking at the blooded ends of my fingers I burst into tears.

'What have *I* done? What have *you* done, more like it. Did you enjoy the show last week? Remember what Rupert was wearing, do you?'

I threw the remnants of the suit at Jane.

The phone rang in Rupert's office.

'Rupert, old man.' It was Martin. 'Rupert, me and Jane have an important dinner party next week, and I wondered whether you would mind lending me that blue suit again?'

Eyes in the Back of her Head

Tara fell to her knees as though she had been shot. Like an unexpected gust of wind, the air whooshed in her ears as the ball missed her by just a couple of feet. She had only that second turned to check the scoreboard, when the bat gave a resounding crack and the cricket ball flew straight towards the back of her head. Her team-mates ran over to help her up.

'You OK, Tara?' said one.

'That was a close call,' said another. 'Lucky you saw it coming.'

'Um, hello, Sophie, she was looking the other way,' said the first.

'I'm fine, no worries,' said Tara, brushing blades of grass from her knees as she stood up.

Combing her fingers through her hair, she smoothed out the chestnut waves so they fell mostly to the back of her neck.

'Still OK for a session in The Toaster after the match?' she asked.

Two thumbs went up, and the girls ran back to their positions to finish the game.

Tara always made a special effort not to get her hair wet in the showers, and today was no exception. She hated to get water in her eyes. Lately, some of the girls had noticed the extra care she took, but Tara was quick to brush off any questions with one excuse or another.

'Good game,' said Sophie as she pulled a sweater over her head onto a still damp body. 'And you were dead jammy not to have been clonked by that ball.'

Tara laughed as she saw that Sophie's sweater had twisted and left her standing with one arm pointing at the ceiling.

'Here, let me help you with that,' she said, turning around to face her friend.

'You two ready, then?' shouted Ruth from the changing room door.

'Coming,' Sophie and Tara sang in unison.

The two girls marched arm in arm towards the door, broke apart for an instant, then joined up again with Ruth as a threesome as they skipped down the broad steps leading from the pavilion. The Toaster was barely two hundred yards from the sports field, and the girls chose a window table so they could watch out for the rest of the team.

'Right, what's it to be?' said Tara, sitting with her back to the counter. 'There's a special offer on double burgers today.'

'So there is.' Ruth stretched her neck to look over Tara's shoulder at the big board behind the counter. 'How'd you see that?'

'Eyes in the back of my head, of course! Mother was always saying she had them when I was a child. I had no idea...'

'So three double burgers with everything, then?' Sophie interrupted, her chair legs squeaking on the stone floor as she stood up.

'Any luck yet with Steve?' Ruth leaned across the table as she quizzed Tara.

'Steve who?'

Steve Steve. How many boys are there that make you drool every time they walk past?'

'I do not drool,' said Tara, wiping her lips with the back of her hand. 'And even if I did, he's never close enough to see it.'

'You're so obvious, Tara. I've seen you do it. When he's in the room, you turn away from him, stare into space like you're on weed and, like, drool.'

Ruth waved her hand in front of Tara's face.

'See. You're doing it now.'

Ruth looked over Tara's shoulder again.

'Oh, got it. He's at the counter.'

Tara ran her fingers through the back of her hair, separating a few strands.

'Anyway, Steve's still seeing Sophie,' she said, looking down at the table.

She could see the counter more clearly now. Sophie slipped her arm around Steve's waist. He pulled her hand away, glancing back at the table by the window. Tara was sure he looked straight into her eye, and shook out the tresses of hair she had just separated.

'Here you go. Special offer burgers as ordered,' said Sophie as she dropped the huge plate of food in the centre of the table.

'Steve's at the counter,' she said, raising her eyebrows. 'Don't know what I've done, but he's being a big shit-hole. I asked him over, but he snapped back at me for the hundredth time this week. You can have him, Tara.'

'You know?' Tara studied her friend's face.

'Everyone knows.'

'But they can't. I won't. It wouldn't work.'

Tara shook her head.

'I'm forever catching him looking at you,' said Sophie.

'Oh, perlease, stop going on about Steve,' shouted Tara.

She jumped up, her legs caught on the table, and the burgers went everywhere. She ran to the door, and the girls watched from the window as she hurried back towards the sports ground, followed by Steve who was rapidly catching her up.

'Watch out Tara,' said Sophie even though her friend couldn't hear her.

'Oh!' cried Tara, as she walked straight into a lamppost.

Her life went into slow motion as she fell backwards, hitting her head heavily on the pavement.

'You OK, Tara?' called Steve as he caught up.

'No, not really, I feel a bit dizzy and my head hurts.'

Steve helped her to sit up.

'Let me take a look,' he said as he moved behind her. 'There's blood in your hair.'

Steve gently parted the chestnut waves. He looked closely at the back of Tara's head.

Her eye gave him a playful wink.

The Last Picnic

The beach huts are padlocked and the only sign of life is a flock of gulls circling overhead, screeching, their dirty white feathers making them stand out against the grey steel skies like smudged charcoal sketches. A long-forgotten kite caught by a telegraph pole flaps hopelessly, cracking with the sound of a whip as it makes a fruitless effort to get away.

Ten years on, I remember how Peter's tears would spill out from his chestnut eyes, then flood across his cheekbones before falling to paint dark circles on an inevitably brightly coloured shirt. Everyone, especially Peter himself, laughed at his jokes.

An arctic wind spikes my eyes and disguises the reason for my tears, but nonetheless threatens to destroy my fragile composure. Memories roll in on the waves and crash like breaking glass against the pebbled beach.

Nine times I have stood on this exact spot. Today, a year exactly after the last occasion, I stand here again and close my eyes.

Nine years ago to the day, Peter had welcomed me with a broad grin, but his words didn't sing as they used to do, his voice flat and underwhelming.

'Just thought I'd surprise you with lunch on our beach, since it's such a beautiful day,' I said, trying to ignore the pain in his eyes.

Peter caught his lips between his teeth and drew a long breath as he pushed himself higher in the wheelchair.

'Right, I'm up for it. Let's make tracks'.

Half an hour after squeezing the folded wheelchair alongside the picnic basket, rugs, beach chairs and medication kit, the horizon abruptly flattened as the sea came into view. I could see Peter's head nodding forward out of the corner of my eye, so parked up gently as close to the beach as I dared. Shaking down my hair, I pushed it back over my shoulders the way I knew Peter liked it and spoke quietly, not wishing to startle him.

'We're here Peter,' I said.

Lifting his head, he gave a deep sigh of approval as his gaze met with the surf creeping up the sandy beach, pushing small pebbles into a tidy line before edging back into the ocean.

It only took me two trips to carry down the beach chairs, rugs and picnic basket. There was no point in trying to push the wheelchair across the shingle. Peter's weight had more than halved even before he moved to the hospice, and my slender frame easily took most of the load. We trod awkwardly over the small stones until he was close enough to collapse into one of the chairs.

'OK if we just sit?' he said, the words coming in one sharp out-breath. Sometimes he was chatty, but today he seemed happy to soak up the energy of the waves, taste the salty tang in the air and hear the whooshing of the surf as it played with the pebbles on the shore.

I sensed that someone was watching us. Peter clearly felt it at the same time, because we turned together towards the road. My breath caught when I recognised the person standing there. An undoubtedly handsome man, neat beard, cropped blonde hair, sports coat and those absurd three-quarter length shorts.

Peter shrugged and twisted back to stare out to sea.

I pressed my hands together and touched the tip of my nose as though in prayer as I tried to fathom out why Michael had followed us to *our* beach.

'Won't be more than a few minutes, Peter. I just want to see why that guy's waiting by our car.'

Peter reached out and touched my arm, his eyes locking on to mine for a second or two before I pulled away.

Scrunching back over the shingle to the road, my legs felt heavier with each step, like trying to run through water.

'Hello there.' I raised my voice hoping that Peter would hear. 'Was there something you wanted?'

Michael smiled as he held out a familiar hand.

'I thought we agreed that this would be my day,' I said, this time lowering my tone.

He put on his silly grin, the one that always worked when I was angry. The grin disappeared as he glanced over my shoulder, and an icy stream spurted through my veins. I swung around to see Peter slumped forward in his beach chair.

'Peter?' I screamed his name over and over as I scrabbled down the shingle, knowing in my heart that he couldn't hear me.

Nine years on, I can relive that day as though it is now. From behind me I hear footsteps in the pebbles, and Michael's warmth breaks my loneliness as he slips a hand into mine.

We watch the crying gulls land on a wooden breaker, perched regimentally, matchstick legs, far enough apart to spread their wings. A sudden bluster of wind forms ashen tops on the waves and the gulls fly off as if in a race, waving goodbye, yelling as they go.

'Peter never suspected anything about us, even at the end. You'd have known,' Michael says, sensing my despair.

But I have never been in any doubt that he did.

Spoiled Pig

Stan lifted his wife's left arm out of the freezer and closed the lid, making certain the catch was securely locked. He smiled as he studied the frozen limb - the gentle contour of the muscles, the slenderness of the wrist, the delicate fingers that had once caressed the back of his neck when they kissed. Placing the arm on his chopping bench, he glanced at the large clock on the white tiled wall. Even after six weeks in the freezer, her watch was still showing the correct time. The watch. A cheap gift from a rep at work, she'd told Stan when he asked.

Had it not been for that watch, Stan may never have worked out that his wife was cheating on him. He began to quiz her about late nights at the office, gifts of expensive perfume, theatre tickets for an evening out with the girls. No, had it not been for that watch things would never have come to a head and she would never have blurted out her lover's name.

Sausages. Monday was Sausage Day. Stan sorted through trays of pork from the walk-in fridge, mostly shanks, a few bellies, the odd shoulder and a dozen less-than-perfectly-shaped chops, all left over from the previous week. He sang sea shanties at the top of his voice as the razor edged knife flashed, separating flesh from bone like ice-cream from a cone. A cleaver thudded on the solid oak block, cleanly cutting an unsold gigot into two.

The arm had started to thaw, and blood was oozing a little from the severed vessels where he had sawn it from her shoulder. He unstrapped the watch and placed it on the counter, took a deep breath, and used his knife to strip the tissue from her bones. Just a few minutes later, he added the flesh to one end of the tray of pork.

When only a pile of clean white bones and gristle remained on the block, Stan carried the tray of meat to the outbuilding which he kept scrupulously clean for joint preparation. He assembled the heavy duty mincing machine with freshly washed parts, and switched on the power. Feeding the pork flesh into the hopper, the machine droned a steady baritone, the note deepening as it struggled with being force-fed the chunks of meat, only to rise again in relief as it managed to force the minced pork through the holes in its stainless steel cutter. Making sure all the pork had fed through the machine, he exchanged the large aluminium bowl of mince for a smaller one and fed in the flesh from his wife's arm.

Stan mixed cereal and his secret recipe of seasoning into both bowls of the minced meat using his hands, combining the smell of the flesh, more pungent now it had been minced, with giddy aromas of country herbs and spicy black pepper. He fashioned two oblate spheroids of sausage meat, one considerably larger than the other. An hour later, he had pumped the meat through his sausage maker into shiny pink skins, linked them while wet and slippery, and hung them on stainless steel hooks above the display trays in the window.

At nine o'clock, Stan lifted the latch on the shop door, and twisted the OPEN sign. The trays in the window were filled with joints of meat, chickens large and small, offal in all its gruesome varieties, and greaseproof bags of dripping, the suet having been freshly rendered while the sausages were being prepared

'Morning Stan. A pound of your best pork bangers, if you please.'

'Morning Joe. I've some special ones here, especially for you. Made them at the crack of dawn, so they are lovely and fresh.'

'Haven't seen the missus for a while,' said Joe. 'Is she keeping well?'

Stan picked twelve linked sausages hanging from the end hook in the window.

'Gone away to be...' said Stan, grinning as his cleaver thudding into the wooden block, slicing the sausage links in half. '...with someone she used to know.'

He slid the sausages onto his scales.

'Exactly one pound,' he said.

'You've been looking after me well lately,' said Joe. 'That liver last week was fabulous. Fried up a treat with onions. So tender. Must have been from a spoiled pig, I reckon.'

Wedding Blues

Jill took her father's arm and snuggled into the sumptuous cream leather seat in the back of the white limousine. She smiled as they pulled away from the house where she had lived since, oh, before her memories began. Old Mrs Juggins waved as they drove slowly past her bungalow at the end of the street and they turned into the main road which eventually led to St Bartholomew's.

Jill looked at the watch that Alan had bought her when they were engaged. Barely half past two, half an hour to go and only two miles to drive. She dared to slip off her white shoes and stretch her toes, letting out a long sigh as she squeezed her father's arm and closed her eyes. In her mind, Jill could see Alan standing at the front of the church, with Reverend Carter watching as she walks along the aisle past friends and family. The organ is playing Pachelbel's Canon in D. Alan turns around and blinds her with one of those smiles that make you tremble inside. Jill sends one back, hidden behind her veil.

'I love you,' she whispered.

'And I love you, too,' replied her father. Jill giggled at the misunderstanding and lay her head back, gazing at the heavens through the sunroof.

'Have you ever seen a sky so stunningly blue? As though it's made a special effort, and swept the clouds under a carpet of trees beyond the horizon. You know, I don't believe I remember it so deep and bright since I was a child, laying in the meadow next to Grandma's cottage, nothing to do but watch for swooping swallows and the white caterpillars left behind by aeroplanes so high they could hardly be made out.'

Jill raised her right hand and gently kissed her grandmother's ring which she wore on her little finger. Something old, she mused, and the dress is new. She had borrowed a pair of silver earrings from her sister, and Mrs Juggins had given her a royal blue garter which she planned to surprise everyone with at the reception. Something blue.

Something blue.

Jill snapped bolt upright. She snatched her arm from her father's, and frantically lifted her dress, sorting through the six layers of white silk laying on her lap. It wasn't there. No garter. No blue. For heaven's sake! She'd put it on early so as not to forget. And only removed it to pull up her stockings. One had laddered, and she had to root about to find a spare pair bought just in case. The garter? Still on the dressing table?

Twenty minutes to three. Twenty minutes. Time to go back?

'Stop!'

The driver didn't. Jill leaned forward and rapped on the glass partition until he turned around. An eyebrow shot up when he noticed Jill's legs.

'Go back!' Jill mouthed.

The partition slid down behind the front seats and the car skidded to a halt.

'You're wasting time. Back. Forgotten something.' Jill could hardly breathe out the words. 'Go!'

The driver looked at Jill's father for an explanation.

'No idea. She lifted her dress and just went frantic.'

The driver's eyes swivelled between his two passengers.

'I've forgotten something. Must have it. Turn around and drive like mad.'

The hedgerows blurred. Jill hurriedly tidied her dress, flicking it down as though brushing off a troublesome wasp.

'It's the garter. I left the garter. How much longer?' Jill stretched to see through the windscreen, her eyes as round as marbles. She checked her watch. Fifteen minutes to three. Fifteen minutes and Alan would be wondering where she was. 'I'm never late. Never late. Never. Ever. Late.'

Hedgerows hastily changed to garden walls, the rumble of the rough country road transformed into a gravelly growl. The limousine braked hard as it turned at the corner bungalow. Old Mrs Juggins waved as they sped past.

Jill was out of the car in stockinged feet and running up the drive even before it came to a stop, her dress held above her knees with one hand and the other stopping her veil from flying off. She turned around at the front door. Her father was puffing loudly as he caught up, wedding shoes in one hand and the door key in the other. He pushed the key into the lock and gave it a twist. Bursting through the front door, Jill took the stairs two at a time.

'On the dressing table,' she pleaded to a non-existent audience as she rushed down the landing to her bedroom. 'Dressing table. Dressing table. Please.'

The garter wasn't there. Perfume bottles, grandmother's silver-handled brush, mirror, hairspray, makeup, tissues. But no garter. Jill threw her arms in the air and screamed.

'Daddy, it's not here!' she shouted, just as her father reached the doorway.

'You haven't called me that since you ...'

Jill screamed again before her father could finish the sentence.

'What was the last thing you remember about the garter?' he asked, trying not to get caught up in his daughter's frenzy.

Jill took a deep breath, and her father cupped his hands over his ears expecting another scream. But this time it dissolved into a burbling sob instead. Jill's chin quivered like it used to when she was a child, and her father almost joined in with his own display of emotion. He sneaked a look at his watch.

'What is it?' asked Jill.

'So what was the last thing you remember?'

Jill flumped on to her bed.

'I really have no idea,' she said. 'I know I took it off to change my stockings and then I put it on the dressing table and if it was on the dressing table I couldn't have missed it so I must have put it back on but...'

'Hey, take a breath,' said her father, and pointed at Jill's feet. 'There's not much time, so you'd best do something about them.'

Jill looked down at the heels in her stockings shredded from running up the drive with no shoes.

'But I need blue,' she said, her chin starting to wobble again.

'You need to get to the Church,' said her father. 'Come on, get them changed and we'll worry about blue on the way.'

Jill opened the top dressing table drawer and pulled out a fresh pack of hose. She opened the packet, carefully removed the silk stockings and threw the cardboard on to the dressing table as she always did.

Hitching up her dress, Jill sat on the bed and crossed a leg. She froze, stock still, then purposefully pushed herself up. Her gaze locked on to the empty packet. Jill picked it up and walked across the bedroom to the waste basket in the corner. Instead of throwing it in, she bent down and lifted out the one she had discarded just one hour earlier.

Underneath there was a flash of Royal Blue.

Full Circle

The church clock strikes seven. A cock's crow pierces the early mist. A body lies across the doorstep of the church, a woollen blanket covering its face. There is a momentary quiet after the seventh chime has faded. A dark grey figure glides past the churchyard wall, before the silence is cracked by a baby's cry.

Silas creaks open his cottage door, wiping a smudge of marmalade into the hoary beard covering his ample chin. He listens, turning his head so his good ear points towards the church, so certain is he that the breeze had carried a child's sob through the old elm resting in the churchyard. A full minute passes before he spits on the step, gives a shrug and shuffles to the garden shed. A shovel, its edge blunted from thirty years of dismal toil, leans against the wall. Silas loads up a wooden barrow and makes his way towards a gap in the wall between his cottage and the churchyard, the gate that used to fill it long rotted away.

Respectfully avoiding the grassed mounds, mostly long neglected, Silas pushes his wheelbarrow past old friends to a patch of ground marked out with twine. He chops into the grass, placing the turves in an orderly heap to one side. Cutting down, his deep breaths savour the earthy tang of freshly dug soil.

'Miss Metcalfe, eh?' says Silas to his departed friends, emphasising his words with downward strokes of his shovel. 'Who'd... have thought... she'd have ended up... like this...?'

The best teacher ever, the children said. Never missed a day of school, their parents said. A second generation of villagers was passing through her classes. The children of mothers who she had taught to read and write, to think carefully about every action, to weigh up the consequences. The locals had it that her most controversial trait was to write the letter i with a circle where the dot should be.

One afternoon when lessons were over, Miss Metcalfe locked the school gate and walked through the village to her home. A few of the villagers remembered waving to her, as they had done for many years, but that afternoon their waves were ignored. Her chocolate box cottage snuggled between two enormous oaks behind a neat hedge of wild roses growing amid a fence of cedar palings. Miss Metcalfe wept as she hung her overcoat on a peg behind the front door.

Although she had taken to wearing loose clothes, a light breeze through a schoolroom window could so easily press the material against her belly. Or a child might hug her in the playground and wonder why they could no longer wrap their arms around her waist. Parents would soon notice that she had stopped walking to the school gate with their children at the end of lessons.

Nobody saw the black saloon draw up outside Miss Metcalfe's cottage late that evening, nor the grey-suited gentleman who got out to open the passenger door.

The queue at the school gate the next morning grew longer by the minute. There was no sign of activity. The wooden entrance doors were closed. The wooden plant stand which at some time would have had a jardinière proudly perched on top in someone's hallway and now served to place the school bell on was not standing at the edge of the playground. Even the window vents in the big schoolroom had not been opened. Children stared through the railings while their parents peered over the top of the padlocked gate. Molly Brown asked another mother to hold her child's hand while she went to see what was happening, and walked quickly towards Miss Metcalfe's cottage.

Everything appeared as it always did. The leaded windows were too small to let much light through, so it was impossible to see inside from the lane. In the windows hung flowery print curtains, the same shade of pink as the roses in the garden, tied back with blue ribbon.

Miss Metcalfe had taught Molly when she was a child, and she felt a little intimidated as she clicked open the latch on the gate. She hesitated, looking both ways along the lane, before walking to the front door. The knocker was much louder than Molly had expected, and when there was no answer she tapped it more gently the second time. Still nothing.

Cupping her hands around her eyes, Molly pressed her face as close to one of the windows as she could. Books were lined up neatly on a couple of wall shelves, a vase stood exactly in the centre of a small dining table on a runner of red velvet, embroidered cushions were puffed up at the back of two easy chairs one each side of an open fireplace, and a brightly polished brass coal scuttle sat cosily in the hearth. But of Miss Metcalfe there was no sign.

Molly followed a thin line of crazy paving around to the back of the cottage. There was no washing on the line, just half a dozen wooden pegs dangling upside down. The grass needed to be mowed, and weeds in the borders were beginning to poke their heads above the purple and white saxifrage which fell across the edge of the lawn. A shock of red hot pokers and proud hollyhocks leaned lazily against the garden fence.

The following day the school re-opened, but it was some months before a gentleman in a black saloon drew up at the school to break the news about Miss Metcalfe's suicide.

His muse broken by a sharp scream, Silas clambers from the grave and shuffles hesitantly towards the entrance to the church. Another squeal. Tiny fingers push the blanket to one side, revealing a neat handwritten note. With a circle over each i where the dot should be.

Life Writing

The Man with a Smile

'Mother, there's no room here for the two of us. I almost dropped the Union Jack on the soldier's heads!'

The tramping of hobnailed boots had lasted for almost fifteen minutes.

'Look, there's Father, elbowing his way into the crowd of officers.'

Margaret waved her flag even more frantically as a photographer captured the moment with a bright flash of magnesium powder, a puff of smoke hovering briefly above his head until blown away on the gentle summer breeze.

'Margaret, calm down,' Mother shouted to be heard above the laughter from the pavement below.

'How can I be calm? Twenty one, and all those handsome young men stopping at our pub for a drink!'

'Margaret Anne Stanhope was born in the late autumn of 1893, into a middle class family of some stature. Her father, a much-respected publican, owned a substantial number of properties as well as holding a considerable investment in equities. So, Margaret, tell us what you remember about those days.' The fresh-faced reporter moved his tape recorder microphone so it pointed across the table towards the frail elderly woman seated opposite.

'Mother always said that the family had ale running in their veins. Not only my father, but also my two brothers, one older and one younger, were in the pub trade. I remember walking through the bars early in the morning with the reek of stale beer, the stench of tobacco smoke and the earthy aroma of a well-trodden carpet playing tunes on my senses. It was as though the voices of the men from the night before were echoing off the brown-stained walls and hanging in the stagnant air.'

Margaret paused, and began to hum under her breath.

'Come on Margaret, give us one last song and we'll drink up and go home to our beds.'

Her trained singing voice hushed the bar-room, locals and military alike hypnotised by the sweetest of sounds, her pretty face, and slim figure. Towards the end of her song, Margaret spotted a soldier writing inside the leather-bound autograph book which had rested on the bar since the beginning of the war. Dropping her arms to her side, she bowed her head to polite applause.

'Thank you, thank you.' Margaret tripped back to the bar, but the soldier had gone. The autograph book laid open at the page he had written on:

It is easy enough to be pleasant when life flows along with a song. But the man worthwhile is the man with a smile when everything goes horribly wrong.

'You know, I still have that autograph book. It reminds me that I found my man with a smile. Robert lived just around the corner, and I knew him as little more than a passing acquaintance at first. We weren't walking out, but frequently exchanged pleasantries, and sometimes his sapphire blue eyes produced a suggestion in my mind which caught me by surprise.'

Margaret's own eyes widened, just for an instant, as she thought back.

'What beautiful roses.'

Robert looked down from his stepladder, pruners in one hand, cuttings in the other.

'Oh, good evening Margaret, how lovely to see you.'

Turning back to the roses, Robert chose a half open bloom and snipped it from the bush.

'This one's for you.'

It may have been some headiness remaining from the bar-room, or perhaps it was the stunning aroma of the roses, or the warm smile that gently creased the corners of his striking eyes that together fired Margaret's passion and dimmed her resistance.

'Perhaps you would care to take some tea, if you have a few moments to spare?'

Margaret looked down at the microphone.

'I remember how his mouth smelled of fruit, how the top of his head was warm to my fingertips.'

Margaret touched her lips.

'1923 was to be the year that my idyllic, rather prosaic life was to become erratic and unpredictable. We married just before my thirtieth birthday, a few months before the child was born. My horrified father bought us a house, I called it our house of exile, in Great Yarmouth, some one hundred miles away.'

'Dotty, stop your nonsense and be quiet for a moment, please. I need to hear what your father is saying.'

Robert slumped onto the settee, the charismatic smile he had gone out with had been left behind at the doctor's surgery.

'He said I have tuberculosis.'

Dotty turned to look at her father.

'What's that?' asked the twelve year old.

'Please go to your room and fetch the sheets from your bed. I need to do some washing,' Margaret lied.

'Probably got it in Europe during the war. He said there's not much he can do, but I have some medicine.'

'But it's only a cough, Robert.'

'The doctor sent me to the hospital for an X-ray.'

The reporter nodded.

'I purchased the burial plot next to Robert's, you know, so I can be with him again when I pass on.'

'So what happened to you and Dotty after Robert died?'

'I had never known poverty. Father always provided well for his family when I was living at home, and although Robert didn't earn a high wage, we wanted for little, because as you know, our house was paid for. After Dotty and I were left alone, we made living frugally into a game and that helped to make the small amount of money we had saved from Robert's pay last for a while.' Margaret sighed. 'But the game became tiresome, and most of our money was soon spent.'

'So you moved back to Bedford?'

'Well, Father reluctantly agreed, with the proviso that I kept quiet about the circumstances surrounding Dotty's birth. My two brothers, one older and one younger, had their own well-established families by then, and Mother was to live for only a further two years. Father died shortly afterwards.'

Deep furrows appeared on Margaret's forehead, and she caught her lips between her teeth.

The solicitor's office was as cold and grey as the morning outside. Framed certificates were all that dressed the magnolia walls, and the furniture was austere with just an old oak desk and a large table. The only nod to comfort was the dark blue carpet, but even that was threadbare in places.

Margaret shivered. It was rare for her to be seated around the same table as her brothers. No-one was talking. They all heard the footsteps outside the door and turned together to watch as the solicitor joined them at the head of the table.

Margaret reached across and touched the reporter's arm.

'Never in my wildest dreams did I ever consider that Father would punish me further, even from beyond the grave. He left me virtually nothing in his will. None of his properties, his business interests or his equities. Just a small legacy and the furniture in the house where I had cooked, cleaned and cared for him.'

'That must have made you very bitter.'

'In a way. But I could understand his actions. What was more difficult to come to terms with was that my brothers, who inherited the lion's share of the estate, didn't even allow me to stay in the big house. Dotty had married and moved away, and I had nowhere to go.'

'Mum, what's the matter? Why didn't you let me know you were coming?' Dotty had no idea that her mother was in such dire straits. 'Come inside, come inside.'

Margaret pushed back the tears that threatened.

'I need to move out of the big house within a few months, Dotty. There will be a little money coming to me from your grandfather's estate, maybe just enough to cover the rent on a small property.' Margaret lost her battle with the tears, and pulled a handkerchief from her sleeve. 'Dotty, would you mind if I moved close to you?'

'Mum, why would I mind? This might be the best thing that could have happened. I was going to surprise you with the news once I knew everything was fine, but there couldn't be a better time to tell you that we're expecting, just before Christmas.' Dotty helped her mother wipe away the tears.

'You mean... you're going to have... you mean... a baby?'

'Two, actually. Twins. And having you living close by will mean that everything will be so much easier. That's if you don't mind helping out?'

Margaret burst out laughing.

The needle on the tape recorder flew into the red.

'Did I mind helping out? It was as though a candle had been lit in a dark room. A flicker of hope for the future. Something special to look forward to. A reason to carry on. Not since I looked into Roberts eyes that evening all those years ago, when he made me feel wrapped up, like an extra-special birthday present, was I so heartened and optimistic about the future. A fresh rhythm and brand new challenges.'

'Margaret Stanhope. Thank you for sharing your memories with us this afternoon.'

Two Minutes Silence

'Your Royal Highness, The Right Honourable Lloyd-George, the Prime Minister.'

Straightening his bow tie, Lloyd-George walked stiffly into the drawing room where he customarily met the King once a week to discuss matters of State. He stood ten feet in front of the King and bowed his head.

'Do be seated, David.' The King waved to the plush velour armchair separated from him by a highly polished walnut coffee table, a wooden ocean between two social classes.

Lloyd-George accepted the invitation with a nod, and made himself as comfortable as his thick woollen three piece suit would allow. Cold weather had arrived early in 1919, and snow threatened even as September was hardly out.

'Sir,' the Prime Minister began. 'You will know from the papers I sent last week that your government is seeking Royal assent to mark the anniversary of the signing of the Armistice with a coordinated period of silent reflection across the nation.'

An aide rifled through the red box on the King's desk and handed over the relevant document.

'And why not a period of celebration, such as was held last year?' As he read the paper, the King raised and lowered his eyebrows, as though punctuating his thoughts.

'There has been much lobbying from around the country to instigate some kind of ceremonial act, and the Cabinet feels that a period of silence would be most appropriate, Sir.' Lloyd-George nodded his head as he finished speaking.

'And how, dear David, do you expect an entire country to coordinate their actions to such a precise degree? Timepieces will show the wrong time, people will be distracted by other events, it would be a muddled insult to our fallen heroes.' The King puffed out his cheeks and allowed his breath to escape with a barely audible whistle.

'Of course, Sir, but...'

'Why, only recently Mother was expected to join us for a garden party to celebrate the sixtieth anniversary of Big Ben, and she turned up an hour and thirty two minutes late.' The King gave a short belly laugh.

'Of course, Sir. However, since you have mentioned it, we had considered broadcasting the chimes of Big Ben over the wireless so that everyone could listen in and coordinate their five minutes silence.'

'Five minutes?' The King sat upright, his hands gripping the carved lions on the end of his chair arms. He thrust his bearded chin forward, his neck resembling that of an old tortoise. 'No-one will stay quiet for five minutes.'

'Perhaps a lesser amount of time, Sir?'

'But then, would it appear to not show sufficient respect?' The King frowned.

'Perhaps three minutes, Sir?'

The King withdrew a large gold pocket watch from his waistcoat.

'Maybe two...' began Lloyd-George.

'Shush.' The King held his forefinger to his lips. 'From... now.' He dropped his finger as though signalling the downbeat to an expectant orchestra.

The Prime Minister watched the King as he regarded his watch, while the aide pretended not to be looking at either of them and appeared to be holding his breath. The velour chair cushion was making Lloyd-George uncomfortably warm and caused him to shuffle awkwardly, and the King threw him a glance of royal disapproval. The aide, whose cheeks were growing progressively redder by the second, took that opportunity to hurriedly take a fresh breath.

'There. Two minutes.' said the King. 'Allow me to consider your proposal and we'll discuss it next week.'

'Sir, perhaps...' started Lloyd-George.

'Eleven o'clock. Prompt.' interrupted the King.

Penny Bridge

The voice reverberated powerfully around the cold stone walls of the little Unitarian church. It seemed to be challenging the pipe organ for authority and winning the battle. Louisa looked over her left shoulder, and a head above the first four rows of the congregation stood a uniformed officer. Louisa stopped singing and stared. Not that a soldier attending church was unusual in 1918, but never before had she seen such a handsome man. Younger than her father, but clearly older than herself. Louisa was spellbound by the thickness of his brown hair, the presidential nose, and eyelashes as long as an artist's brush. But what struck her most was the way he stood. Head stretched towards the rafters, one arm bent neatly behind his rod straight back, the other holding a hymn book level with the medals on his tunic. Although the book was open, the soldier was not reading the words. His eyes were firmly fixed on the minister as he blasted out the hymn with a formant worthy of an opera singer.

With no warning other than two or three flat notes, the sound from the organ began to fade.

'my heart and... tongue confessed,' the congregation stuttered.

Louisa twisted her neck so she could see the organist. He was still playing, even though the only sounds were clacks from the keyboard.

The minister began the next verse.

'Yet, Lord, Thy saints...'

Louisa was his only accompaniment, her voice fragile and hesitant. Then, unexpectedly, the soldier picked up the tune.

'...some profit by the good we do.'

The minister smiled a sense of relief as the congregation followed along with the hymn.

The organist, who had quickly vanished behind the organ, reappeared and nodded to the minister before resuming his position in front of the pipes. The organ, quietly at first, but then more forcefully, made it through until the end of the service.

The minister shook the soldier's hand warmly with both of his as he left the church.

'I cannot thank you enough, sir.'

'Really, it was nothing Father.'

'Your voice saved me a great deal of embarrassment,' insisted the minister. 'The organ has been faulty for weeks, but even in Cambridge we have suffered the austerities of war and cannot afford to have it repaired.'

'Perhaps I could look at it?'

'But you must be passing through. I would remember had I heard your voice before.'

'Just returned to London lodgings after three years in Belgium, and decided I should visit your university town before settling back into a civilian role. I'm a master printer by trade, but have trained in engineering. Really, I would be delighted to look at the organ for you.'

The soldier hesitated.

'Except...'

'Is there something you need?' asked the minister.

'Well. I am booked on a late train back to London this evening. Wasn't planning on staying over, you see.'

'That, sir, is not a problem. I will ask the verger to accommodate you overnight. Allow me to introduce you.'

The minister beckoned Louisa and her father over.

'Walter. This is... ,' then turning to the officer, 'Sorry, but I didn't ask your name.'

'Brooks. Cameron Brooks. British Army. Second Lieutenant. Pleased to meet you. And this is?' Cameron nodded towards the young woman.

'Louisa, my daughter.'

The verger stepped forward, his arm outstretched, but Cameron had already reached for Louisa's fingers and kissed the back of her hand.

'I am charmed to meet such an astonishingly beautiful young lady.'

Louisa clasped her hands together and looked down at them, her bonnet hiding the redness of her cheeks.

Since the window looked out at the main street, Louisa closed the curtains in the spare bedroom before switching on the pale electric light. The walls were hung with a dowdy paper, tanned stains above two redundant gas lamps. None of the furniture matched, but the walnut wardrobe, dark mahogany tallboy and an oak wash stand had proved adequate for the few visitors who stayed over. The double bedstead had an incongruous wrought iron headboard which Louisa secretly hated. Secretly, because her father had bought it specially for her. A threadbare rug rested next to the bed, breaking up the stark wooden floorboards.

The door clicked open, and Louisa turned to see the handsome soldier closing it behind him, gently but firmly.

'Oh, I won't take long. I've made up the bed with clean sheets. I'm afraid it isn't the most comfortable, though.'

Cameron brushed Louisa's sleeve as he walked to the bed and pressed down with both hands to test the mattress.

'That seems fine, thank you... Louisa.'

'Father said I was to make sure you have all you need, sir.'

'Please, Louisa. Call me Cameron.'

Louisa felt her knees weaken as he said her name, his voice no longer distinct as it had been that morning in church. His words were instead running together like melting candle wax.

'May I fetch you anything, sir? Some hot milk? A nightcap? Perhaps...'

Cameron touched Louisa's lips tenderly with the tip of his forefinger and let it rest there.

'You must call me Cameron, Louisa. I will have it no other way.'

Louisa's hands were shaking. She wrapped them around Cameron's fingers, pressed them softly to her mouth, and closed her eyes. Barely uttering a sound, Louisa mouthed his name against his hand.

'Such a beautiful young lady,' Cameron said for the second time that day.

'Cameron,' she whispered, parting her lips to taste the warmth of his fingertips with her tongue.

Louisa opened her eyes as Cameron slowly moved his hand to touch the side of her neck. She knew he would feel her heart beating strongly as he bent forward and kissed her on the lips.

'Cameron, no,' Louisa breathed, pulling away.

'Anything I need, Louisa. Remember what your father said.' Cameron's liquescent voice enflamed her deepest desires.

'No, Cameron. Please.'

Cameron kissed her again, and Louisa felt his tongue urgent against her lips, his body crushing against hers until her every nerve ending trembled like a feverish child.

Louisa rarely rose early enough to catch the moon peering between the towers of the old college buildings, but to reach Westmorland and their new home before nightfall they had to catch an early train. Following a final check on the suitcases, giving Vaughan his first feed of the day, and preparing Cameron a hearty breakfast, they were at last ready to leave for the railway station. Louisa paused for a moment at the front door, just in case her father might concede and bid them goodbye, then closed it quietly.

After struggling through swarms of students rushing to their colleges, the station booking hall offered some degree of sanctuary. Louisa took a deep breath and exhaled noisily through pursed lips. With a conciliatory shrug of her shoulders, she relaxed to the warm tone of muffled conversation, interrupted only by the occasional clicking of heels on the stone floor.

'That was quite a walk, Cameron. I'll sit while you buy the tickets if you don't mind.'

Cameron nodded, dropped the suitcases next to an empty bench, and jostled his way to one of the ticket office windows.

Louisa watched the crowds coming and going through the huge arched doorway leading to the concourse. She was hopeful that her father might change his mind and decide to see them leave for their new life with his blessing, but there was no sign of him.

'At least he allowed us to stay until you were born,' Louisa spoke softly and smiled even as a tear fell from her cheek on to the small child in her arms.

'I have the tickets, Louisa. You look strained. Are you feeling unwell?'

'No. Thank you. I just wondered if Father might have reconsidered.'

Louisa pulled Vaughan tightly to her chest as she felt more tears threaten her composure.

'Platform 5 for northbound trains, apparently,' said Cameron, picking up the suitcases and striding across the hall with Louisa close behind.

The steady throbbing from the wheels mixed with the blurred hedgerows had mesmerised Louisa, her eyes wide as they stared, unseeing, from the carriage window. She blinked as the scenery turned to black, as suddenly as if someone had placed a hangman's bag over her head. The dim electric lamps, set centrally above the bench seat on each side of the carriage, were just bright enough to make out Cameron's reflection in the window. Vaughan stirred, disturbed by the different sound from the track.

'Do you know where we are?' Louisa asked, watching Cameron's image in the window.

Cameron moved the newspaper closer, concentrating to read in the faint light.

'Any idea where this tunnel is?' Louisa turned from his reflection to face her husband. 'Cameron?'

'No idea, Louisa,' Cameron replied, rattling the newspaper noisily.

Louisa looked back to the dark window, the light from the carriage just enough to cast a soft glow on the tunnel wall. She wondered if perhaps her father had been right.

Louisa heard the flap on the letterbox snap shut, dried her hands and went to pick up the post. Just one letter.

'Cameron Brooks,' she said out loud.

She turned the envelope over, but there was no return address. Just a Keswick postmark.

Louisa held it against the sun streaming through the kitchen window, but couldn't make out anything but the postmark.

'Who do we know in Keswick?' she asked herself.

Pressing the envelope to her nose, Louisa breathed in deeply. A faint scent. Faint, but familiar. Familiar enough to make her raise an eyebrow. Just a little. Placing the letter behind the egg timer on the dresser where it would be easily spotted by Cameron, Louisa returned to finish the washing up.

Drying the final plate for much longer than was necessary, Louisa stared thoughtfully at the pile of crockery before laying her cloth on top. She walked to the back of the kitchen, opened the door to the stairs and made her way to their bedroom. Opening the third drawer down in Cameron's chest, she moved his clothes carefully to one side, taking out his favourite blue cotton shirt. The shirt she had washed and ironed the day before. Raising it to her face, she took a deep breath, breathing in the faint odour. There it was. Weak, but unmistakeable. The same as that on the envelope. Violets. Sweet violets. Not the flower. Those little blue sweets that women keep in their purse to freshen their breath. Louisa carefully refolded the shirt, and placed it neatly back in the drawer with the others. She sat on the edge of the double bed. The one she shared each night with Cameron.

'Violets. Who does Cameron know in Keswick who would smell of violets?' she mused.

The cottage door banged open, jolting Louisa from her thoughts.

'Louisa. I'm back. Forgot my wallet.'

Louisa ran to the top of the landing.

'There's a letter for you,' she shouted. 'Behind the...'

The cottage door slammed shut. Louisa walked down the stairs into the kitchen and checked the dresser. The letter had gone, but the soft hint of violets lingered.

'I was chatting to Freda this morning in the greengrocer's, and she said she'd seen you in Keswick. Last week.'

Louisa rattled her tea cup on its saucer and looked across the table at the back of Cameron's newspaper.

'Hmm,' Cameron mumbled from behind the paper.

'Keswick. Were you in town alone?'

'Hmm.'

'Cameron.'

'What?'

'Last week. I didn't know you'd been to Keswick.'

'Business. I was there on business.'

'You usually say.'

'Spur of the moment. I had a letter asking me to meet up. You remember. It came just the other day. You left it behind the egg timer.'

'What's her name?'

Cameron let the top of the newspaper fall forwards so he could see Louisa.

'Her?'

'Her name. What is it?'

'You mean Mr. ....'

'Does he always write letters that smell of violets?' Louisa interrupted.

'Perhaps his wife used the writing pad.'

'Your best shirt has smelt of violets on and off for months. I wash it out best I can, but it comes back. When you've been away on business.'

Cameron threw down the newspaper.

'It's Melda, isn't it?' asked Louisa.

'How do you know her name?'

'You mention her. Quite a lot. In your sleep.'

'That means nothing, Louisa. Nothing. You're making something of nothing.'

'Freda said there was a child with the woman. The one she saw you with in Keswick. A boy. About five years old. Said you picked him up. Twirled him around. And kissed him. On the face.'

'Donald.'

'Donald who?'

'Donald is Melda's lad,' Cameron looked down at the crumpled newspaper. 'Fine boy he is, too.'

'What's he to you?'

'You really don't...'

'Cameron, tell me,' Louisa interrupted. 'Why would you kiss him?'

She paused, then with a slow shake of her head continued.

'He's yours, isn't he? He's your son?'

Cameron looked up at Louisa, and they locked eyes, each refusing to be the first to look away. Finally, Cameron averted his gaze to the floor.

'He wasn't planned. I paid a brief visit to Keswick to see the family the day I returned from Belgium.'

'Not planned. Like Vaughan wasn't planned, I presume?'

Louisa's voice quivered.

'Melda lived next door. My parents were out. She asked if I'd like some tea. One thing led to another...'

'Just as it did in Cambridge.'

'I was tired, weary of the trenches, drained from the wretchedness of war.'

'And Melda helped ease your troubled mind.'

'Just as you did in Cambridge, Louisa. Just as you did.'

Cameron held out a hand.

'Forgive me, Louisa. I had no idea about Donald until last month. Melda was forced to get in touch as her mother died and she had no money to continue renting their cottage.'

'So, you are paying her keep...'

Louisa spat the words across the table, and hesitated before continuing.

'...and Melda rewards you in what way?'

Cameron jumped up from the table, his chair flying backwards across the floor. He yanked his jacket from behind the door, swinging it open to bang against the wall before turning round to face Louisa.

'So now you know. The children have a half-brother. Is that such a terrible thing? I still come home to you each night. That must tell you something?'

'It tells me you're happy for me to cook your meals, clean your clothes and comfort you in our bed, while you are spending time away with another woman.'

'A month, Louisa. A month.'

Cameron stormed out of the cottage, a triangle of light falling across the path all that was left behind.

Louisa poured the boiling water into the teapot, swirled it around until the pot felt warm, and emptied it down the sink. The door latch clicked and Cameron appeared, unsteady as he walked into the kitchen.

'You stink of ale,' Louisa said, spooning tea leaves into the pot.

'Ale this evening, violets earlier on. Is there no limit to your observation skills Louisa?'

Cameron exhaled like a deflating balloon as he fell into a chair.

'You didn't close the door,' Louisa sighed as she walked across the kitchen.

'Louisa,' Cameron grasped her arm as she passed his chair. 'Louisa, there's something you should know.'

The door creaked open a little wider to reveal a woman clutching the door frame, the lower buttons on the front of her coat unfastened, making a poor job of concealing her bulging stomach.

'Sorry Louisa. I said she shouldn't come. Found me in the tavern. Followed me home.'

The woman seemed to crumple a little, and Louisa caught her arm before she could fall. A familiar smell caused Louisa to furrow her brow.

'Melda, I presume. Why are you here?' Louisa asked coldly.

'Why do you think?' Melda looked down at her ample belly. 'Take a guess. It's due next month and I'm not going through that a second time without the father by my side.'

Louisa backed away from the door, her eyes sparking angrily above flushed crimson cheeks.

'A second time? You mean...' Louisa hissed.

'You already know about Donald, I'm sure. We plan to live as a family.'

'But Cameron already has a family,' Louisa cried. 'And he only just found out about Donald.'

Melda laughed and had to catch her breath before replying.

'Only just found out? Is that what he told you?'

Cameron, no longer quite so fuddled from the ale, pulled himself upright in the chair.

'He's been paying towards Donald for years, since he was born. I was sure you must have known, what with him visiting so often. Sometimes he seemed to spend more time with us than he did with you.'

'Cameron, this isn't true,' Louisa interrupted. 'Tell me she's lying.'

Louisa shook her head, slowly at first, then faster as she realised Cameron wasn't going to reply.

'No... No... No.'

Each time Louisa uttered the word it increased in pitch and volume, the final time sounding like a knife had pierced her heart. She sobbed so much she could barely speak, until anger took over.

'The weekend business trips. Cameron? You said you had to go otherwise you'd lose your job. And the nights you were held back because you were so busy at work? And the times you missed the last train home?'

The lines of Louisa's brow deepened, as she spluttered the words.

'Her? You were with her? Tell me. Tell me it's not true.'

'I'm sorry, Louisa,' Cameron started.

'You're sorry? Then, after spending time with her you'd come home to our bed and... and... as though nothing had happened?'

'You've been well looked after, Louisa. As have the children. None of you have wanted for anything. And Melda is the one with another child on the way.'

'But Cameron,' began Louisa, her hand sliding down to her belly, 'She's not the only...'

"Not the only what, Louisa?' Cameron interrupted. 'Not the only woman to find comfort in my arms? Not the only woman to conceive my child out of wedlock? Not the only woman to find me attractive? Indeed she is not, as you are well placed to know.'

'I know. I do know, Cameron. But... you are choosing her over us?'

Louisa's mouth twisted in grief as Cameron walked across to Melda and wrapped his arms around her. Melda buried her head against his chest.

I drop the latch with the softest of clicks. This is the last time I shall hear it. Pushing the door gently with my fingertips, it feels secure. I turn my back on the cottage and my two darling children, warmly tucked into their bed thirty minutes ago. Although I had sipped only the smallest glass of sherry, I have to catch the trellis arch to compensate for a slight headiness. A rose thorn scratches the back of my hand as I draw it away, but I don't feel any pain. Taking the half dozen steps to the garden gate, I glance towards the village church.

Turning away from the church, I can feel the cool night breeze bring a colour to my face which I neither want nor can control. Forcing myself not to look back at the cottage, I take a few paces along the rough stone path towards the centre of the village. As I'd expected, and indeed prayed for, everyone is indoors. An infant's cry causes me to look up at an open bedroom window, and I remember that I have deserted my own babies. But I'm too weak to change my mind, and pause only for a few short breaths outside Mrs Jenkins'. The soft light from an oil lamp flickers, like a fading flame, behind pretty floral curtains.

My body shivers. Every part of it. I tell myself it's the cool air and gaze upwards, searching the stars for strength. Sucking in their magnificent splendour warms me sufficiently to continue my journey, and I drag my aching heart away from Mrs Jenkins' cottage. The moon hangs low in the night sky, appearing large as it peeks boldly between the hills just as it used to in Cambridge so far away in distance and in time.

Carried through the valleys on a gentle breeze, I hear the last train of the day sound its whistle as it leaves Ulverston. I hope the children don't awaken before Cameron manages the long walk from the station. But there is nothing I can do to change things and, like a runaway engine, my destiny is sealed. My pace quickens; it matches the pounding rhythm of my heart.

The blush of the moon gives precious little light, and I falter slightly as the footpath ends and I step down onto the road. Looking first towards the village, where I left my babies, then to the shadowed lane leading to Penny Bridge, I remember the first time we walked from the railway station to our new cottage. Five years ago. Five years. Hopes still high, dreams yet to be dashed, plans so far intact. A gate clicks closed behind me.

The reek of tobacco offends my nose as I approach the grey concrete bus shelter. I know that I'm halfway to Penny Bridge, having walked the route and measured the distance in footsteps a dozen or more times in the past four weeks. I slow a little and peer inside. The glow from a cigarette end illuminates the faces of two dark figures sitting on the bench. They call out for me not to tell their mam that I'd seen them.

The fork in the road where I shall turn right for Penny Bridge is lit by a shaft of light shining through the partly open door of the house on the corner. My instinct is to knock and tell about their daughter smoking cigarettes in the bus shelter, but as quick as the thought occurs it vanishes, like a breath in mist on any icy morning. I'm sure I feel something move in my belly, but it is surely too soon and definitely too late in equal measure. I hasten past the house, taking hurried steps towards the bridge, the murmur from the beck getting louder as it flows over raised cobbles.

The moon has hidden its face behind a cloud as I reach the bridge, and I struggle to make out the stile which I must cross for the footpath that leads down to the beck. This is my final hurdle. I look across at the tavern the other side of the bridge where the road rises and curves away in the near distance, and listen to the dull rumble of conversation tumbling from an open window in the bar. They are in a different world. One that will see the dawn of another day. They will return to their homes, eat supper and go to their beds. I toss the thought around in a sea of contemplation, my mind a small boat in an ocean so vast it has no horizon. For an instant, the notion of walking back to my cottage calms the crashing waves, but with the tranquillity comes the recollection that my decision is made.

Once over the stile, nothing can get in my way. Lifting my skirts, I climb over the timbers and make towards the beck. My shoes feel as though they are sticking to the grassy path as I place one foot in front of the other. I kick off the shoes, but my feet are as heavy as my heart and it makes no difference. As I reach the water's edge, speckles of light from the inn reflect in the wavelets, twinkling like stars in the night sky. The beck is not as cold as I thought it might be. I lay down and lower my head, tears falling heavy until my eyes touch the surface. The burbling becomes muffled as my ears fill with water. I take a small sip, then a longer swallow, then another. But it isn't my thirst I am here to satisfy, and breathe deeply until my sorrow drowns.

Micro Fiction

Rescue Me

My breath was not coming easily as I lagged further behind. The rest of the group had disappeared round a crag, their voices no longer a comfort. I thought to blow the whistle. Three sharp peeps they said. But I wasn't in trouble. I thought perhaps to catch my ankle in a cleft. That would be an emergency and I could blow the whistle.

The mist fell fast over Tryfan, and even as I turned the crag there was only cool clammy silence ahead. My eyes bulged as the gloom threatened to suck them from their sockets. Was that a shadow? 'Hello?' I turned around. The mist had thickened and the outlook was the same whichever way. I drew out the whistle and sucked a breath, holding it longer than planned. 'Hey!'

Startled, the whistle fell from my icy fingers to clank tunelessly along the scree at my feet. The slap across my cheek caught me by surprise, and I dropped to one knee. Although thick material, a sliver of shale penetrated my trousers. Standing up, I wasn't sure if the wetness was blood or damp from the ground. The whistle was close by, and as I stretched to reach it a boot thudded on my hand. I felt my little finger crack, and screamed.

At last, I could blow my whistle.

Greasy Spoon

Forty years of eating fry ups. Not just fry ups, but fry ups with lard. Touch a match to his greasy hair and he'd likely burn like a candle. The kids love him though. They have no idea. I've told him over and over. Please don't serve them breakfast. Does he listen? Do they? We need a good breakfast to get our brains in gear for a day's learning, they say. Please give them scrambled eggs instead of frying them, I asked. Give them toast instead of a fried slice. Grill the tomatoes rather than have them spitting around in a pan. Use low fat sausages. They *ain't natchal*, he'd say. Well, Mr Greasy Spoon, have you never looked at your eyes in a mirror? They have yellow spots. You know what they are, Mr Greasy Spoon? Cholesterol. And you know why, Mr Greasy Spoon? Because you eat lard. You know what lard is, Mr Greasy Spoon? It's pig fat. Subcutaneous fat from a pig. And you know what happens to that pig fat, Mr Greasy Spoon? It soaks through the wall of your intestines into your blood and charges around your body looking for places to coagulate and create problems. In your case, Mr Greasy Spoon, it doesn't have to look far, does it? I do my best for the kids. They get the best books I can afford, the best teachers I can find, the best sports facilities. And you, Mr Greasy Spoon? What do you do? You fill their stomachs with pig fat.

Faith

'Higher,' he called. His daughter peered at him through the branches. Whenever she saw his laughing eyes, she could do anything, climb forever, up to heaven if needs be. Her father had taught her she could even fly if she believed. She waved and clambered onto another bough, then another, and another. The trunk was getting thinner, and the limbs became branches. She could just make out the cottage at the end of their road. The tree moved in the breeze, swaying like when her father held under her arms and swung her from side to side. She closed her eyes. 'Higher.' She couldn't see him for leaves, but could feel the warmth of his broad smile.

One more step upwards. Little more than a thick twig, the next one snapped with a loud crack under her foot. She tried to grab the trunk but toppled forward and fell through the tree, arms outstretched, the twiggy bits scratching red lines on her cheeks as they swiped past her face. A broken branch hooked the hem of her pretty peach skirt and stemmed her fall for a second until ripping free, sending her tumbling head over heels. A final limb caught her under the belly and she bent in two, winded, before it broke and she carried on earthwards.

Her father had taught her she could even fly if she believed, and her spirits were soaring as she struck the ground with a sickening thud.

Haggis Supper

Moira never knew her real parents. They died in a road accident driving home from the hospital after her birth. Moira was thrown from the car, and survived the fire which had engulfed her mother and father. Raised by her grandparents, she was an awkward child. Her early years were plagued by a succession of complaints from her class-mates' parents over her strange behaviour and at senior school she was a frequent target for bullies.

Moira's grandfather died in unexplained circumstances when she was fifteen, after which she left home and scraped by in a bedsit, earning money flitting between waitressing jobs. Marrying Iain changed her life. He was cultured, handsome, and had a fabulous career in the city. But it was not only Moira who was attracted to him, and three years after they were married she discovered the evidence.

Iain didn't know she'd found out until too late. Moira finely chopped the daffodil bulb and threw it into the pan with the minced offal, oatmeal and suet. He died in agony, just as Moira's grandfather had done.

Doggone

Sitting on a squeaky and half collapsed wicker basket filled with stinky rags, uneaten cheese sandwiches and half empty bottles of fizz-less lemonade, I turned my head and stared into the face of the most miserable-looking dog I had ever seen. Never could there have been a more despondent, dejected and unhappy face than the one this dog was wearing.

Scrabbling around the bottom of my basket, I found a packet of biscuits I'd dropped in before leaving that morning. The transformation was incredible. Instant. One second misery and despair, the next moment glee and laughter.

We would have made a great comedy double act. Looked at each other, then we looked at the float, each other, the float, each other, the float. We tried to vary the time interval to catch the other out, but without exception when I looked at the dog, he was looking at me, and when I turned away he did exactly the same.

He was still laughing when all of a sudden he dashed off along the bank. I watched him until he disappeared round a bend in the river, and that was it. My companion had grown tired of my company.

I was despondent, dejected and unhappy.

Sisters

'Izzy?' I whispered her name. A cool whirl of air gently kissed my cheeks. 'I know you are there.'

The curtains sucked inwards and cracked a little, allowing through a streak of yellow ochre from the late setting sun, their movement a signal that the front door had opened. I held a long breath and listened for the telltale squeak from the staircase. As soon as it came, I exhaled with a long hiss, so long I thought my lungs might collapse. I had to press down hard with my belly muscles to keep from panting.

I watched the doorknob twist, threw my head back on the pillow and squeezed my eyes tightly closed. My right hand ached with holding the knife, and I let go to wipe my damp palm on the sheet. Wrapping my fingers once again around the handle, I pressed the cold steel against my thigh.

The mattress moved, and I knew from the smell of stale beer that his mouth was barely inches from mine. My eyes flew open, and although the room was in twilight I could make out the cocktail of iniquity and sick desire in his expression.

'Isabella.' I moved my lips, but without uttering a sound. 'This is for you.'

CCTV

With the last cable plugged in, the television screen flickered into life. A silver estate glided silently past the house, Mrs Drummond from two doors away dragged her shopping trolley home from the supermarket, a youth on a bicycle held up two fingers to the camera as he rode along the pavement. It didn't get more exciting than that and I nodded off.

The brakes squealed as we slowed into Ambleside station. Steam hissed from underneath the carriage. The engine sighed, relieved to reach the end of the line. A compartment to myself, I released the leather strap and dropped the window in the door. A cool draught against my face broke the dream.

I hit the rewind button. Cars drove in reverse and pedestrians did silly walks. Mrs Drummond waddled backend first to the garden gate and looked towards the house. She put her hand on the latch, seemed undecided, then shook her head. I chuckled as she walked home the wrong way round. A youth with a grey flat-cap pulled down at the front walked backwards up the garden path struggling with the weight of what looked like a microwave oven. Twice he left empty handed and repeated his neat trick of walking backwards to the house, this time with a shopping bag.

Same make as mine.

Freedom at Last

Life at home was claustrophobic, dull and restrictive, and Grandma's spare bedroom looked so inviting. I could help out with caring for her and at the same time enjoy the freedom that every young girl dreams about.

October, with its shortening days, saw Grandma closing her curtains earlier in the afternoon and opening them later each morning. She occasionally asked if I would mind keeping her company now that the evenings were drawing in. My friends understood. After all, when I was at home, my parents often told me I couldn't do that, or I couldn't go there. But this was different. I was grown up, left home, my own boss. So of course I didn't mind spending the occasional evening, maybe two, with Grandma. Mondays and Wednesdays, and sometimes Thursdays, became regular card sessions.

Friday was club night, and one week Grandma must have heard me singing in the bathroom as I dolled myself up for an evening at the Glitz. She made me jump as I opened the door. The singing had reminded her of some old records she'd been keeping under the stairs, and would I like to play some of them? I glanced at my phone, checked the time, and told her that would be lovely. How could I not?

Grandma pulled the heavy velvet curtains tightly closed.

Number Four Cake

'If you're happy and you know it clap your hands.' Teddy clapped his hands. Mummy said I could have a number-four-cake for my party. There was a red fire engine and we couldn't get to the number-four-cake shop. I saw a lady looking funny with a cape round her and wet hair and shiny things sticking out her head like in a comic. A posh girl with a pink handbag and pink skirt and pink top had a pink shoe on and a blue shoe on, and Mrs Brown from up our street was stood there with a wire basket and nothing in it.

'There was a little bunny who lived in the wood. He wiggled his ears like a good bunny should.' Teddy wiggled his ears. Mummy said hello to Mrs Brown from up our street.

'I'm a little teapot, short and stout. Here's my handle, here's my spout.' Teddy put one hand on his hip and held the other one out sideways.

Mrs Brown from up our street laughed at Teddy. I just looked at her back. And she wasn't coming to my party.

Teddy stopped being a teapot and Mummy must have missed that Mrs Brown from up our street was just in front and pushed the buggy right in the back of her fat legs.

'If you're happy and you know it clap your hands.' I laughed, and so did Teddy.

The Green Man

When Desmond was a child, he liked to make paper planes and launch them from his bedroom window. He wanted to be a pilot. Really desperately wanted to be a pilot. He eventually discovered he couldn't. Colour blind. Courtesy genes from his maternal grandfather. He was a signaller in the Great War, so why couldn't Desmond fly planes? Colours aren't that hard. Yellow is sun, blue is sky on a summer's day. Brown is darker than red, green is lighter than both. Orange is yellow but darker, and violet is a dirty blue. Desmond squinted his eyes to check the shade of brightness. No-one ever asked him why. At school he painted pink cats, green cows and purple rivers. No-one ever said to his face. In the science laboratory he got the litmus tests results correct half the time. That was good enough to scrape through. Desmond trained in electrical engineering. He matched colours against a crib sheet kept in his pocket. No-one ever knew. He bought green tomatoes and unripe bananas. His meat was always overcooked just in case it was still pink. Friends thought he was a bad cook. They criticised his dress sense, and said his tie didn't go with his shirt and his socks didn't match. Desmond waited for the little man on the pelican crossing to turn green and walked across in front of a lorry. No-one knew why.

By the same author:

Whomerley Wood Moat, Stevenage
- The House in the Clearing

WHOMERLEY WOOD MOAT
STEVENAGE

THE HOUSE
IN THE CLEARING

Philip Wadner

Believed to have been the home of the de Homeley family in the late thirteenth century, the site of the medieval moated homestead in Whomerley Wood, Stevenage is located about one and a half miles almost due south of the original Saxon settlement around where St. Nicholas Church stands today. Evidence of medieval life has been found there, and excavations on the island have also uncovered relics from Roman times. The author has sifted through a huge variety of sources, and has knitted together facts, suppositions and his personal reflections to create a powerful image of times gone by.

Probate - A Personal Journey

After a sad family bereavement, I started out on what I thought could be a lengthy and arduous process of obtaining probate, not least because that is what the legal profession would have us believe. It was not. There were hiccups, of course, but none of any great consequence. The process didn't take long, and it was not expensive. Anyone of reasonable intelligence, who can use a computer, write letters, keep accurate records, and understand official guidance should be perfectly capable of obtaining grant of probate and administering an estate.

This is a diary of what happened to me. It is not a typical 'How To' guide, but is a record of my personal experience.

I hope it will encourage others to take the plunge.

www.ingramcontent.com/pod-product-compliance
Lightning Source LLC
Chambersburg PA
CBHW071350170626
46811CB00003B/1066